THE CHEAT

Also by Robert Dietrich

Be My Victim
One for the Road

The Steve Bentley Thrillers

Murder on the Rocks
End of a Stripper
The House on Q Street
Mistress to Murder
Murder on Her Mind
Angel Eyes
Curtains for a Lover
Calypso Caper
Curtains for a Lover
My Body
Guilty Knowledge

As Howard Hunt aka "E. Howard Hunt"

Stranger in Town
Dark Encounter
The Violent Ones

THE CHEAT

ROBERT DIETRICH

CUTTING EDGE

ISBN-13: 978-1-952138-63-8

Published by
Cutting Edge Books
PO Box 8212
Calabasas, CA 91372
www.cuttingedgebooks.com

1.

WHILE HE WAS STILL SLEEPING the woman left his bed, pulled her dress down over her lean body, brushed her hair with brief, nervous strokes, and left the room to go across Paris to the apartment where her husband slept. The dress was one her husband had chosen for her at a Molyneux showing, but now it was rumpled and slightly torn at the shoulder. The woman was tall and her jet-black hair had been touched with red lights by the sun of Deauville and Antibes. As she walked through the empty *conciergerie* to the sidewalk, she felt the chill of the Paris dawn and shivered.

Waiting for a taxi she held her arms closely to her breasts as guilt and shame came into her mind and she acknowledged them for what they were. As often as she had slept with Robert Webster she had felt the same way afterward. She could not accustom herself to infidelity even though she knew her husband was not in love with her. The guilt she felt was because she had not loved her husband when she married him, and she did not love him now. As Hildreth Kaufman got into a taxi, she lighted a cigarette, sat back and told herself it was better to go to bed with a man you wanted than with a husband you did not love.

Frederic Kaufman did not hear his wife enter their bedroom. The windows were open to the Avenue de Wagram, and early traffic noises covered the sound. He slept soundly, without dreams, the uncomplicated sleep of a man without problems. He was the Paris partner of a New York investment house, and he had eaten an excellent midnight supper at La Rue with his mistress after losing his wife at a party they had arrived at together. Losing Hildreth was not a rare occurrence any longer; it had come to be a game between husband and wife at which they took turns, and last night it had given him the opportunity to send a car to Passy for Suzette and dine with her in a *cabinet particulier* at La Rue.

His wife sat down softly on the edge of the bed, glanced at the shadow of stubble on his face and put her cigarette between her lips. She rolled down her stockings carefully, dropped them onto the carpet and pulled bed covers over her naked body. After a while she stubbed out the cigarette, closed her eyes, and listening to the regular breathing of her husband, she fell asleep.

The door buzzer sounded in the apartment of Robert Webster. He woke slowly, thinking it must be Frederic. It must be Hil's husband, and as he turned to waken her to hide, he saw that she was already gone. So the quick reaction he had felt subsided, and he put on a dressing robe and opened the front door.

The man who had wakened him was a letter-carrier with a letter sent by *pneumatique,* and when Webster had given the man a tip he closed the door again and walked to the window to open the letter. The engraved return address on the envelope said *Cygne Productions, Kress-Gringold, 52, Ave. Champs-Élysées,* and he tore open one end to pull out the letter it contained.

A check was enclosed and he looked at it before he read the letter, feeling pleased at first that the money had come; then, when he saw the check was written for only sixty thousand francs, he began to read the letter without pleasure.

His eyes skipped over the typed words until he understood their meaning and then he crumpled the letter into a ball and threw it toward a corner. The same evasions; the same citing of delays in getting distribution for the film he had written for them, and now, instead of the monthly payment agreed to, only a third of that. They had done the same thing to him last month and the month before. They were strangling him with their failures and their problems and their hand-washing excuses for not paying him, and he felt like picking up a chair and smashing it against the wall. He felt hatred for them corporately and individually because they had brought him to Paris and worked him for five months writing and re-writing a picture for which Webster gradually had lost the slightest hope of commercial success, and instead of paying him six thousand dollars they had said they could pay him only one hundred and eighty thousand francs a month until the picture was released and money began to return.

He ran his hands across his face, feeling the rasp of his beard, the angry pulse in his throat, and looked down through the window at the Boulevard Raspail below.

It was too late to go back to bed again, and still too early to find breakfast in a café. Walking past the bed he looked at the vacant side where Hildreth had slept, and wondered why she had not stayed longer. In the small kitchen Webster measured coffee-chicory into a percolator, added water, and placed it over the gas burner. In his breadbox were a few dried slices of French bread and two molding *croissants*. He emptied the breadbox into the wastebasket and walked back into his living room. He found an almost-empty package of cheap Gaulois cigarettes on the coffee table, and lighted one, inhaling slowly to lessen the impact of the smoke on his lungs. He coughed a few times, grimaced at the cigarette, and began pacing the living room floor.

As he walked he noticed the two cognac glasses from which he and Hildreth had drunk late last night, and the after-taste seemed to fill his mouth like cotton steeped in stale vinegar. That had been the end of the cognac, he remembered, and he would have to buy a new bottle before Hildreth came again. The room was neither a garret nor the well-kept suite of a hotel; it was a furnished apartment in the Sixth Arrondissement of the kind let to Sorbonne students with money, or to couples with only a retirement income. It was luxurious in comparison to some that Webster had seen where other Americans tried to live like Frenchmen, but it. was only a shabby cell in comparison to the suites at the "Joe Schenck"—the George Cinq—where Kress and Gringold maintained themselves on money that was not theirs.

He heard the water begin to boil over the burner, and frowned at the thought of the breakfasts that would be served to Kress and Gringold at the Joe Schenck. They would have wine-soaked melons from Morocco, pots of thick black coffee, flaky *croissants* and balls of Normandy butter. A black Renault sedan would be waiting for them at the hotel entrance when they left for their office sometime before noon, and they would be smoking mild Dutch cigars and American cigarettes.

He thought, they can live that way because they're spending money they owe me. I signed the contract with them in America, in Hollywood, U.S.A., but it doesn't mean anything over here. Even if I could afford to hire a lawyer to sue them, they could pay for a better one with my money and I wouldn't get what they're sending me now. They hired me because they couldn't get anyone else to fall in with their scheme, and I signed with them because I hadn't worked in nearly a year. They could have bought me for half of six thousand bucks and I would have paid my own passage, besides. But now I know all about them and they know all about me. Independent producers they call themselves, but that's only another name for confidence men. I gave them their picture in spite of everything they wanted to change; I showed them how to cut down on production costs; I saved them the capital investment so they could make a profit sooner. Like a damn fool I was considerate of them, and if the picture ever shows a profit it will be my fault. But now they've got what they wanted out of me; they've got their picture. It's up to them to get the distribution outlets they said they had. That part is out of my hands. I don't pretend to be a promoter so I can't help there. What I wanted was a picture good enough to give me a new chance, but they've seen to that. The last time I saw the picture I thought about asking to have my name taken out of the credits, but I didn't because I was afraid they might stop paying me anything at all. So I kept my mouth shut and prayed.

The coffee was percolating over the gas burner, and Robert Webster went into his kitchen to watch the brown liquid spurt and bubble against the glass top. Before he lifted the pot from the flame, he thought, if I hadn't needed rupees plenty I might even have let them pay me in stock. If I had done that I would have a number of engraved shares in an unreleased third-grade motion picture and a gigolo job at the Bal Tabarin.

He poured coffee into a cup, opened the kitchen window and took a half-empty bottle of milk from the outside sill. He poured a little milk into his coffee, grimaced when he saw it had turned sour, and carried his cup into the living room. He sat on the sofa stirring sugar into the coffee, rested his feet on the low table, and began to plan his next interview with Kress and Gringold.

When Frederic Kaufman opened his eyes there was sunlight in the bedroom and he saw a strand of his wife's hair on his pillow. He wondered when she had come back and it pleased him that she had. He could not remember the circumstances that surrounded their parting the night before, other than that when he had run out of conversation with some silly person he had looked for Hildreth and not found her. His fingers lifted the strand of dark hair from the pillow and toyed with it as he debated whether to wake her. He liked the color and the feel of his wife's hair, and even its smell. Frederic Kaufman was glad he had married an American girl who took frequent body baths and did not place all of her confidence in a *bidet.* He let the strand slip from his fingers and raised himself on one elbow to look at his wife's sleeping face. He decided that she had come back sober to their apartment because her face looked washed and her lips were without lipstick. If she had been drunk when she returned she would not have bothered to wash her face and scrub her lips. Her bare upper arm was near him and he kissed the flesh delicately, then waited. When the kiss did not waken her he looked at her regretfully and sat up to get out of bed.

Lighting a cigarette, he inhaled carefully—as though the least sound would waken his wife—and put slippers on his feet. He was wearing broadcloth pajamas—a gift from Suzette—but like many American women, his wife slept nude. Frederic knew a great deal about America and its fauna; he had graduated from the University of Pennsylvania where he had studied finance, and where he had learned that a man who dressed well and spoke English with an interesting accent could make a substantial impression when such an impression was desirable to make. He was fond of America with its well-bathed women and its ready money, and during the war years he had maintained an intimate contact with both. By good luck he had been in America on business when Pétain submitted to Hitler, and he had stayed there during the war years and returned to Paris soon after its liberation with a wealthy wife from Chicago.

The sound of traffic on the Avenue de Wagram was increasing, and Frederic Kaufman thoughtfully closed the bedroom windows. He drew the blinds so that Hildreth could sleep as late as she cared to and walked into the bathroom. Turning the tap for his bath he began to review his schedule for the day: a transatlantic call at eleven-thirty; lunch at Le Cercle with an undersecretary of finance; tea in the Bois with Suzette and a late afternoon appointment with those two imposters, Messrs. Kress and Gringold. They were thieves, those two. Really they were, brigands. They would want more money, of course—they always did—but this time they would go away empty-handed. Their picture was finished, at last, and ready for release. Soon they would have to pay back the loan with interest and everyone would be friendly again.

Frederic Kaufman tested the bath water with his toe, increased slightly the flow of hot water, and got out of his pajamas.

Before he stepped into his bath he opened the door a crack to see if he had wakened Hildreth, but she was still sleeping. One of her arms lay across the pillow he had vacated and her eyes were still closed. As he settled himself in his bath he wondered whom she had picked up the night before—some new fellow, or the same one she had been sleeping with the past three months?

As Hildreth Kaufman slept, a dream came into her mind and she saw herself as a girl in Evanston on a Sunday afternoon, waiting to go to a polo game at North Shore with a boy from Northwestern. She saw the boy's face again, smooth-skinned and virile with deep-set, brown eyes that could make her heart melt when he looked at her. That afternoon had come nearly twenty years ago, but she always saw him as a boy of twenty-one with a Cord roadster and a tweed motoring cap, and in her memory he would never age. Her dream was one that came to her many times each year because after the polo game was over he had driven her to a roadhouse outside Des Plaines, and by the time he brought her back to Evanston she understood what other girls at the Parker School talked about in whispers between classes.

Over the years the memory of pain had vanished, and she could only remember the touch of his hands and the sound of his voice and the strength of his arms, even though she had hated him defensively and cried each night for a month until she was sure nothing else was going to happen. Because she had been sure she loved him, she had gone to Northwestern for one year to be near him, but when he graduated and married another girl, she had left Northwestern and gone to Pine Manor in Wellesley, Massachusetts.

The dream made her stir restlessly, and when her husband came out of the bathroom he saw her hands open and close as though she were trying to recapture something that had vanished.

When the dream left she did not dream again. She never dreamed of her husband because he was not a romantic man as she had supposed all French men to be, but an intensely practical man who taught her how to make love correctly, remembered her birthday and their anniversary and brought frequent remembrances from Cartier's to demonstrate his fondness for her. Hildreth's father had introduced her to Frederic when Frederic had come to Chicago from New York to see her father on a business matter. The war was nearly over then and Hildreth longed to go to France with an attractive husband and spend the rest of her life at Eden Roc or on the Lido. She had never seen either, but she knew girls who had and she was sure that Europe would be an exciting place to live. So she had made herself and her father's money attractive to Frederic Kaufman who cooperated by asking her to marry him and promising her a pleasure-filled life in the ballrooms and salons of liberated France.

Post-war France had disappointed her, and she spoke French so poorly that she preferred to see Americans or those French who spoke understandable English. When she had seen Mont St. Michel, the chateaux of the Loire, the beaches and forests of France, and the *boîtes de nuite* of Paris, she found her life at a plateau, open in all directions, but attractive in none. Even the discovery that Frederic was keeping a mistress brought no more than a momentary impact to her emotions; the fait accompli opened to her an avenue of retaliation that she had only occasionally considered. Frenchmen of her acquaintance were willing, provided they did not depend upon Frederic for their living. Then there were the young American executives and lawyers who represented American firms in France, an occasional diplomat, a traveling correspondent, a sculptor, a magazine photographer, and ultimately, Robert Webster, the screen writer.

Hildreth had met him first on the set of a picture which was financed by her husband's investment house. In an effort to alleviate her boredom, Frederic had arranged for her to see the filming of the picture, but he had never visited the studio himself. She had liked watching Webster work with the actors, improving their lines, adding business to a scene, swearing when the day's shooting ran into overtime, and she had felt sorry for the look that came to his face each time Kress or Gringold made a change in the story.

When the picture was finished there had been a party for the cast at the George V, and somehow she had found herself with Robert Webster. Both of them had felt sad because the picture was finished, but to Hildreth it meant an end of a daily routine, a place to go. Because they felt sad they got drunk together and left the George V for Montparnasse and a series of Existentialist *caveaux* where no one had ever taken her before. Because she was drunk and grateful and because she had become very fond of Robert Webster she spent the night with him at the Hotel Lutetia, and in the morning she was pleasantly surprised to find that she had become even more fond of him. Each week since then she was with him two or three nights even though he had moved out of the Lutetia to a shabby flat because he was having trouble getting his money from the producers.

Her sleep was nearing its end, and as her husband adjusted his bow tie in the mirror, he watched the muscles of her face move slightly as though she were trying to speak. He thought once more of waking her, but her face relaxed into a mask of calmness and he shrugged his shoulders in defeat.

Brushing the lapels of his coat, Frederic Kaufman decided to escort his wife to a good restaurant for dinner that night. He admired her face and her body and he knew that other men admired her equally. He enjoyed seeing their admiration when his wife was with him, and he felt that in some way it reflected personal credit to him.

A little before noon Robert Webster took the *Metro* at Raspail to the Place de la Concorde, changed to the Élysée line and got out at the Rond Point stop. Before leaving his flat he had shaved and put on a clean shirt. He wore flannels, a fairly new tweed coat and an English tie with regimental stripes. Walking toward the Étoile he saw a bootblack and stopped near a *pissoir* while his shoes were shined. The sidewalk crowd was beginning to thicken as men and women left their desks and their offices to eat lunch and walk in the warming sun. As he watched, he thought, this could be Broadway at noon, or Vine Street or Geary Boulevard or the main street of any big American city. If you half-close your eyes there isn't any difference at all. It isn't until after dark that the streets of Paris change into something that nothing else can match. The magic doesn't come until night.

He gave the bootblack thirty francs, lighted a Bleu and turned into the entrance of Number 52. Taking the elevator to the third floor, he stepped out and walked down the hallway to a door with a black silhouette of a swan and the legend: *Cynge Productions, Kress-Gringold.*

Webster looked at his cigarette, decided whether to throw it away or keep it, and decided to keep it. The hell with Kress and Gringold if they didn't like his coming in with a cigarette between his lips. It was a lousy Bleu anyway, with tobacco as dry as October leaves, and he hoped the smoke would choke them. He pushed open the door and walked to the reception desk where Hélène was filing her nails with an emery board. She put down the emery board and stretched her hand away to look at it.

Webster said, "I don't suppose they're here yet." He sat down in a leather chair and looked at her.

"It is still early, Monsieur Webster. They have not come and I do not know when they will come. Perhaps not until the afternoon."

"What's their hurry?" he asked bitterly. "They've got all their problems solved."

Hélène shrugged and picked up the emery board to round off an offending nail. "Today they have not called even one time. Do you want to leave a message for them?"

Webster took the check from his pocket and held it toward her. "I got this early this morning."

"*Oui.* I sent it myself to you by *pneumatique* so you would have it today."

Webster looked at the check again, then at the receptionist. "You made a mistake," he told her.

"A mistake? The bank would not cash it?"

"I haven't tried. You could cash it right now with the change in your purse. It's only a third of what it ought to be."

She shrugged. "I made it out for the amount they said. Are you sure it is not correct?"

Webster put the check back inside his billfold. "I'm sure," he said. "If they've got enough money to live at the George V, they've got enough money to pay me for writing the picture."

Her eyes opened innocently. "But I have understood that an arrangement was made..."

"It hasn't been kept."

She held out one hand, and said, "Do you wish to leave the check here? I will show it to them when they come."

Webster laughed shortly. "I'm cashing it before they decide to stop payment. But they owe me two more like it."

"And that is what you wish me to tell them?"

Webster nodded. "If you can remember a complicated message like that. They can send both checks in one envelope and save postage." He ground out his cigarette in her ashtray.

Hélène's eyebrows arched, and she smiled cooly. "I am sure they will make their distribution arrangement today. Or perhaps tomorrow. In any case, they will surely give you what is coming to you."

"I wish I shared your confidence," Webster said. As he stood up he saw Hélène open a desk drawer and take out an envelope. She handed it to him, and said, "This letter came for you this morning."

He took it from her, said thanks, and went out of the office. He walked down the hallway slowly, wondering whether he should have waited in their office or whether he should try to see them at the George V. Screw Hélène. Her superiority was the kind that came from sleeping with her employer. She had big breasts and a big behind and she wanted to act in a Kress-Gringold production. Webster rang for the elevator and told himself the only production she was likely to be starred in would be an intimate one behind the locked door of the Kress-Gringold office with one or both of her employers in a feature role.

Futile as the exercise had been, Webster felt better for having gone to the office. Part of his anger had been jettisoned on Hélène. She knew he was being cheated, but the knowledge meant nothing to her other than a sneer at him because he was dependent upon other men with whom she was intimate. She was a type he had known in Hollywood—the offices of the world were filled with women like Hélène who lacked the courage to be full-time whores.

Walking down the stairway he thought of going to the George V to see them, but decided against it. If they were there they would be able to avoid seeing him, and he would have wasted his time.

Well, his day had been wasted so far, like so many other days before it. He wanted to spend one day in Paris that was not wasted. Just one. That would be the day when he got his money and bought a cabin-class ticket back to New York. He had waited a long time, but he could see no end to the waiting.

He looked at his watch, crossed the Champs and took a sidewalk table at Le Marignan, his back to the tall plateglass windows. He ordered a *fine café.* Drinking it, he watched the thinning sidewalk crowds, listened to the scrape of feet against the sidewalk and the honk of klaxons in the Avenue. It was a super, end-of-summer day, neither hot nor chilly, and the chestnut leaves were still a fresh green. He tried to put Kress-Gringold

Productions out of his mind, and began to think, instead, of Hildreth Kaufman.

Because she had come to him last night, he was reasonably sure that she would not come tonight. There was a rhythm to her visits that seemed to move her in his direction at intervals that must be conditioned as much by her husband as by her own desire. For him the afternoon was free, and the night. He remembered the letter that Hélène had given him. He took it from his pocket and saw that it had been addressed to him in care of Cygne Productions. The address was written in an old-fashioned script, and he tore open the envelope.

Dear Robert,

Just recently I read that you were making a picture in France, and I decided that it would be nice to see you again.

I've been living here since my granddaughter, Tay, won a fashion prize. She works in the *Madame* offices in your building and supplied your Cygne address.

If you could possibly do so, please come to my atelier for tea on Tuesday afternoon.

Sincerely,
Lydia Crandall
(Mrs. John F. Crandall)

He turned over the envelope and saw that the return address was on the Place du Tertre in Montmartre, and then he put the letter back inside the envelope. He remembered Lydia Crandall very well. She was the grandmother of Lee, the woman he had once married. Lydia was the matriarch of the Pasadena Crandalls and he had been fond of her. Even after the divorce from Lee he knew that she did not blame him alone.

He remembered Lee's younger sister as a girl of nineteen or twenty who had been East at Bennington most of the time he had been married. Tay had her sister's chestnut hair and a good figure, and Webster could not remember much more about her.

Putting the envelope back into his pocket, he decided to see Lydia Crandall tomorrow afternoon. It would be interesting to find out what had happened to the Crandalls in the last six years.

2.

HILDRETH LAY IN A WARM BATH, scented with Swiss pine oil, reading the Paris edition of the New York *Herald Tribune.* She was a little angry with Frederic because he had gone to his office without saying goodbye to her, but she understood that he might be irritated because she had left him so abruptly the night before. Dropping the newspaper onto the marble floor of the bathroom she closed her eyes and leaned back so that her head rested against a soft plastic pillow suspended at the end of the tub.

She remembered last night better now. Frederic had been trapped in conversation with the wife of a Marseilles merchant. She herself had left the party so quickly that she had forgot her mink stole. Perhaps Frederic had remembered to bring it back with him. If not, she could send for it today. There had been a jolting taxi ride to the Boulevard Raspail, and four dark flights of stairs to Robert's flat. He had not seemed surprised to see her, and had made coffee for them, with cognac afterward, and a little later they had gone to bed. She could remember undressing in front of him, watching his eyes as she discarded each article of clothing, feeling shamed, yet exulting in what she did; wanting to be everything to him that a *poule* could be; forcing herself to an aggressive coarseness that disturbed and stimulated her.

She liked Webster's short graying hair, his regular features and his eyes. Their calmness attracted her and gave her confidence in their relationship. She knew that Webster had been married and she wondered whether the woman had given him up willingly. It did not matter that he had only a little money; she already had everything she wanted, but it would be nice if she could go away with him for a month to Hendaye or Juan-les-Pins before the season ended. He danced well, drank well, and she wanted to see him lying on a beach tanning his body under the sun. She knew that he could not really afford to take her anywhere until he was paid by his producers, but she could easily pay everything for both of them. It would be nice if she could persuade him to go.

Opening her eyes she looked at the outline of her body under the tinted water, at her submerged breasts that rose free of their own weight, and she was pleased with what she saw. Her right hand pinched together the flesh of her belly and there was no slackness of muscle and no fat. She knew that her body had reached its ultimate perfection and that from now on she would have to be ceaselessly careful lest it begin to deteriorate. Her loins were soft but firm, and as her hands passed through them she thought again of Robert Webster, wondering what he was doing at that moment.

It was her husband who had awakened her body and taught her its endless exploitation, and she did not understand why he made so little use of it now in their life together. She envied his mistress somewhat, but by now she was accustomed to the arrangement and she knew that she would show bad taste in questioning the situation after so long. After a while she sat up, took a razor from the soap well and began carefully to shave her legs.

Tay Crandall sat at her desk and pushed aside a litter of fashion sketches received by *Madame* during the day from dress houses in Paris, London, and Rome. She had taken notes on the best of them, and tomorrow she would show them to the lay-out department for an analysis of the page space allotted to her description and comments. She was tired and the day had come to an end. Outside and below, the Champs-Élysées was becoming a traffic artery, bottlenecked at the Étoile, with cars fighting to free themselves and head toward Auteuil, Neuilly, and La Muette.

Along the Champs a few shops had lighted their windows but the street-lights were still dark, and for a moment she saw the Champs-Élysées as through a silk screen, gently lighted and posed, and beyond the rooftops and the Seine, the outline of the Eiffel Tower burned red by the hidden, setting sun.

Then it seemed as though the silk screen was taken away and the set darkened, and in a little while the street-lights went on in a long chain of diamonds that stretched away to the Place de la Concorde. The cars below turned on their headlights to make a current of moving lights that milled around the Étoile like schools of phosphorescent fish.

When she looked away from the window she saw that the office was nearly dark and most of the women had left. The clack of a single typewriter echoed through the big room, and a light burned above a drawing board where someone still worked. Her eyes were tired and her body felt heavy. She stood up, turned off the desk lamp and thought for a moment of Robert Webster. She wondered what he would look like when they met tomorrow at Lydia's. When he had been her brother-in-law he had been handsome and aggressive and a wonderful dancer, and she remembered that she had probably been a little in love with him. But just as a girl, she told herself. He'll probably be old and dissipated now and won't even remember me. If he does he'll still think of me as a little girl; he won't realize that I've grown up.

I never really knew about the divorce. Lee didn't want to talk about it, and I was away at school, so all that I heard was family talk. But Lee told me once that he was good in bed, so I know that hadn't anything to do with it. Or running around with other women. It wasn't like that.

Anyway, tomorrow evening I'll see him again and I suppose just seeing how he's aged will make me feel old, too.

As she began to adjust her hat, the telephone on her desk rang. The sound echoed through the room until she picked it up and answered.

The voice was one she had been half-expecting to hear, with its Mediterranean softness and British public-school overtones.

She said, "Hello, Rino. Where are you?"

"Still at the damned machine shop, darling. Drive-shaft won't balance."

"The Ferrari?"

"Of course the Ferrari. I'm driving it in the *Rallye*."

"Yes."

"No point in staying here. I'll wash up and meet you."

"How soon?"

"Say an hour."

She nodded as though he could see her. "I'm awfully tired tonight, Rino. I hope we can make it an early evening."

"We don't have to go if you don't want to."

"No. The Ambassador's a friend of yours."

"Yes. I love you, darling."

"See you in an hour."

"You love me, don't you?"

"Of course."

"Be cheerful, then. What's the good of being in love if one can't be cheerful."

"I am cheerful," Tay said, her eyes searching the darkened, deserted office. "I'm afraid I'm just tired; that's all."

"*Ciao,* darling."

"*Ciao,*" she said, and placed the telephone receiver back on her desk.

When she had crossed the Champs, she took a taxi to the Place des Saussaies because darkness had come and she was too tired to walk.

In her apartment she got into a warm tub and closed her eyes to rest them. Next year she should really start wearing glasses. Otherwise the corners of her eyes would begin to wrinkle and she would look older than twenty-six. This was one evening that her grandmother would not telephone and insist that she come to her studio for supper and a long evening of talk about painting and family friends in Pasadena and Santa Barbara.

The tepid water relaxed her body, draining away its weight and its tiredness, and she began to feel that she would be able to walk back through her bedroom without collapsing across the bed and going to sleep. Rino would want to come back to the apartment with her, listen to opera records for an hour or so and then make love to her. It was how so many of their evenings had been since she had known him, and she realized that it was as routine as marriage and probably as unexciting. Rino Menotti was the only Italian who had ever made love to her, and she had found him exciting at first, and amusing, and because of him Paris had become a city that vibrated with life and beauty. He was wealthy enough to do nothing but race the expensive cars he owned, and she assumed that he was brave. His face was handsome and sensitive, with light-olive skin; white, even teeth and black hair that curled sometimes just in front of his ears and over the silk collar of his shirt.

She believed that in his way Rino was in love with her, and for a time she had been in love with him. But she was not enough in love to marry him, even if he did not have a wife and children who lived with his father in Genova. More than women, Rino Menotti loved automobiles, and because he did not live purposefully, as Bennington had encouraged her to live, it was a small barrier between them.

Drying herself in front of a mirror, she posed for a moment, the towel caught between her legs and draped across her right shoulder. She had upswept her hair to bathe, and with her knee bent slightly her pose was Grecian. Then she pulled the towel across her shoulders and walked into her bedroom to dress.

A friend had brought a bottle of Australian whiskey to Webster's flat, and they were working through it methodically. The friend was a Frenchman named Roland Perrex who had directed the filming of the screenplay that Robert Webster had written. He shared Webster's view of the disaster.

The windows of the flat were open and they could hear the night noises of the Boulevard Raspail. During the war Roland Perrex had worked at De Gaulle's headquarters in London and he spoke good English. Because he was a Gaullist he had found it hard to find post-war employment in an industry so closely controlled by *franc-tireurs.* Perrex hoped that he would be able to get another assignment before his last picture had been shown to the public.

Webster lighted a Bleu and looked out of his window at a cyclist who was pedaling along the Boulevard four stories below. From somewhere there came the sound of singing that was smothered by the rasp of klaxons at a distant carrefour. He said, "We ought to have our own company, Roland."

Perrex shook his head. "I've tried it before, but they are very shrewd students of the franc, these *banquiers.* If we had one good picture behind us we would have no difficulty in finding money for another. But then we would not need outside backing. It is a very vicious circle. *Un cercle vicieux.*" Perrex lifted his glass to Webster. He drank briefly, and said, "The whiskey is corrosive. I apologize for it."

"We can go somewhere and buy a bottle of good wine to take away the taste."

"And later, perhaps, a girl or two?"

"Not if they want presents."

Perrex took out a small notebook and leafed through its pages. "There are always certain young ladies who aspire to motion picture employment. Under such circumstances presents are unnecessary. Such an arrangement would interest you?"

"No." He poured whiskey into Roland's glass, and added the last of the Vittel. "I'm going to try to work tonight."

"Very commendable. A screenplay, perhaps?"

"I don't know what it will be. Maybe just a story."

"Very well. I am moved toward revelry this evening, and I regret that you cannot accompany me," Perrex said, and stood up. "If I am to have any choice at all I must begin telephoning at once."

"Good hunting."

"Thank you. I am confident of success." He went out of the room and closed the door behind him.

Robert Webster opened the case of his portable typewriter and brought the machine to his coffee table. He put a sheet of paper under the roller and flexed his fingers.

I've gotten this far before, he told himself, but always late at night when liquor had relaxed my brain and ideas could flow; always late at night, or in the morning when I was hung over and too tired to keep writing more than a couple of hours. Or Lee would cut into my thoughts, complaining that she was lonely and why couldn't we go down to Mike's for a couple of hours, just to be seen; and when we got back it was useless to try to weave the threads again because by then they were withdrawn and sheathed like severed tendons and everything I had written had to be thrown away because the good thoughts were gone.

In school I had to work to keep my scholarship. I read my texts and I made my grades because I had to, and always inside me there was a drive to do well and excel wherever I could. I didn't let down and I didn't let anything interfere. It was having a goal that kept me at work, and when the thing with Lee turned bad the goal was gone.

But I haven't written myself out yet. I settled for the easy and the obvious, the thing that was in demand, and I write my screenplays and my originals, knowing always that they're never quite the best things I could do; and I even got an Oscar, but when I wanted to do an honest story for Paul Gringold, he made a perversion of it that can't possibly deceive anyone.

He looked at the sheet of paper in front of him and thought, there won't be any Lee to interrupt today. Nor a producer, nor even a friend.

In his mind a sentence was born and then a paragraph and beyond it a sense of mood that shaped itself into a plot. He shifted the typewriter to the left margin and began.

In two hours of writing his mind was steeped in the creation of a story, and he began to feel the old, accustomed sense of satisfaction as he thought about the story. Its people moved through his mind, acting their parts as clearly as though he were seeing them on the screen of a private projection room. They had body and depth, and integrity, and to him they were unquestionably real.

He lighted a cigarette and as he dropped the match into an ashtray he saw Hildreth Kaufman open his door and come into the room.

She dropped her fur stole across the back of a chair and walked toward him. He stood up, mechanically, to greet her.

"Surprise," she said. "Frederic is out somewhere with his *amoureuse.* I said I was going to the ballet."

He looked down at the page in his typewriter to fix the place in his mind, and then he said, "You didn't call, Hil. I didn't think you'd come."

"I hope you aren't angry. I knew you'd be right here." She looked down at the typed sheets of paper on the coffee table. "I'm so glad you're writing again, darling. You're so frightfully intelligent you simply mustn't get rusty." She picked up the top sheet and began reading it. As she read she began to frown. When she had finished a paragraph, she laid it down, and said, "I guess I just don't understand it, darling. It doesn't sound at all like you."

"So it might just be good." He offered her a cigarette but she made a moue and took one from her handbag.

"Simplify things for me, darling. Just tell me about it."

He shrugged. "I don't tell a story very well."

"You've never talked to me about your work, Web. Is it because you think I wouldn't understand?"

"I haven't done much to talk about." He watched her sit in a chair. "Want me to make coffee?"

"Not unless you were going to. But I could always use a drink."

Webster went to the kitchen, made two drinks with Roland's Australian whiskey and tap water, and brought the glasses back. She sipped her drink and looked at him across the rim. "Cheers," she said. "Success."

Webster drank with her. "I've had the cheers. I need a little success."

"No. What you really need is a few weeks on the Riviera, darling. To relax and get perspective."

He nodded. "I won't argue."

"I'm tried of Paris; fearsomely tired of being wifely to Frederic. This is such a wonderful time of year to be on the Mediterranean, Web. We could even go down to Spain if you like."

Webster said, "I can't go, Hil. You'll have to go without me."

She sat forward and reached out to hold his hand. "Please, darling, I want us to go together. Just the two of us. We could have a month in the sun we'd never forget the rest of our lives."

Webster drank from his glass and looked at her. "All right," he said. "When do you want to leave?"

Her face brightened. "As soon as I can develop a domestic cold that only the Riviera sun can cure."

He looked at the stained wallpaper of his flat. "Suppose you go on alone and I'll come down as soon as I've finished what I'm writing."

She frowned slightly. "Will it take very long?"

"A week."

"A week from now?"

"Yes."

She leaned forward so that she could kiss him lightly. "This is our chance for a little happiness. You'll never regret it." She leaned back, crossed her legs, and exhaled smoke through her nostrils. Her eyes closed, and Webster wondered what she was thinking. He found himself looking toward his typewriter.

He said, "Frederic will know why you've gone away."

"I suppose so. But he might even be grateful. He's having those tedious talks with Paul and Henri again."

"About my picture?"

She opened her eyes. "I don't think so. He may even finance another picture for them."

"For God's sake, why?"

"Why should you care, darling? If Frederic lends them money for a second picture, they should be able to pay you for their first."

"I thought your husband was a smart businessman. His money hasn't come back yet from the first picture. Doesn't he know it isn't good business to back them a second time until the first picture has paid off?"

"I really don't think it's anything you ought to worry about. It's Frederic's problem completely. And it might help you get your money." She came to him and sat down beside him on the sofa. "Can we talk about our trip now?"

He kissed the side of her face. "Where do you want to go?"

"I've thought of Guéthary or Bilbao. Then there's St. Tropez, Hyères and La Ciotat and lots of other possibilities. Why don't I find some comfortable place and wire you where to come? Ever since yesterday I've been praying we could do it together."

"Praying, Hil?"

She colored slightly. "Well—you know what I mean." She turned so that when she lay backward it was across his thighs, and her hands bent his head down to hers. Almost before their lips met he felt the serpentine darting of her tongue, and then her body arched, pressing against him, and he heard her shoes tumble onto the floor. As he leaned away to turn out the typewriter light she stood up quickly and pulled her dress over her head and he was surprised to see that the single motion had made her naked.

Under his hands her breasts swelled, and as she opened her thighs her loins were soft as suede. Her arms formed a circling cable around his body and she began to moan unintelligibly.

He was too unprepared to respond other than mechanically, and although it was deep and thoroughly complete for her, Webster found only a shallow and momentary calm. She left him to go to the *bidet,* and when she came back she turned on a light and pulled the fur around her naked shoulders. "You're good for me," she said. "Wonderfully, tremendously good." She sat in a chair and straightened her legs in front of her. "Does it please you to have me say that?"

"Yes."

She lighted a cigarette and exhaled smoke along the length of her body. "I need you, Web. I need what you can do for me. I need what I can do to you. Without it I think I'd go crazy."

"You wouldn't."

She glanced down at the meeting of her loins, and said, "No. In time I'd find someone else and make the adjustment. But I don't want to try."

"No."

"You can't guess how much it means to me to come here like this and be with you. You really can't begin to guess."

"I think I can," he said. "Do you have to talk about it?"

She shrugged. "I don't have to; but I want to. That's part of it for me. Talking about it afterwards. I guess you'd like me to put on my clothes now and go home."

"I don't mean that. Only talking about it isn't the same thing."

"It's part of it, darling. There's a beginning and an end. Always. Please don't be delicate."

"All right." He sat up, ran his hand through his hair, and looked at his typewriter. If he let her talk awhile she might get it out of herself and go away. Then he could get back to work.

She stretched her body as though she were awakening, and then she said, "The first time we met, Web, did you think you'd sleep with me?"

"Yes."

"How disillusioning. What made you think so?"

He shrugged. The conversation was tiring him. "The way you walked, your face, the kind of body you have."

She smiled as though she were pleased. "Then I'm not really to blame. You didn't even think I might be a chaste wife?"

"No."

"Not ever, Web? Not even for five minutes?"

"No," he said. "Christ, no, Hil! When a woman wants to get laid it's stamped across her face in red. Then everything she says or does becomes a pattern."

Her smile disappeared. "It wasn't much of a chase for you, was it?"

"Why should it have been? We're old enough to do what we want without being coy."

"Well," she said, thoughtfully. "I suppose so. I just don't think I was as obvious as you thought I was."

"Hil," he said, "I was probably wrong. The thought didn't even occur to you until we were in bed together." He got up from the sofa, collected their drink glasses and took them to the kitchen. In Roland's bottle there was only enough whiskey for two thin drinks. Webster made them, and carried them back to Hildreth. She had not moved from the chair and she had not put on any more clothes.

She looked up at him, and said, "Kiss me, Web."

He leaned down to kiss her. Then he walked back to the sofa. She watched him reading the page in the typewriter, and asked, "Was your wife blonde or brunette?"

"On the redheaded side. Chestnut hair."

"Was she beautiful?"

He took a deep breath. "Yes, Hil, she was beautiful. She had big breasts, a superb body and she made love like a mink."

She did not notice the tone of his voice. "What was her name?"

"Lee."

"She must have been extraordinary, darling. Why were you and she divorced?"

"She talked too much. She didn't know when to keep the *bouche* tightly closed." He drank deeply from his glass and looked at his mistress. "Hil, don't act insulted. I gave you the answer your question deserved. There must be things to talk about that don't include the ex-Mrs. Webster."

Hildreth's face had gone a little slack. She sat forward, her knees, bent, and then she stood up. "Let's talk about me, then." She began to walk toward him.

He felt her hands behind his head, pulling his face against her belly.

"Are brunettes better than redheads?"

He felt deadly weary. "It's the woman, not her pigmentation." He looked up, along the fur, at her face. "Why talk like a fool, Hil?"

"Because I am, I suppose." Her hands released his head, and he sat back, gratefully. "I *am* a fool to come here and be treated this way by you."

"I thought you liked it."

"Yes. But I'm still a fool. If I were a little more of a fool than I am I'd let myself fall in love with you. Would you like to have me in love with you?"

"It isn't necessary."

She stepped into her shoes, steadying herself with one hand on his shoulder. "No, it isn't necessary. Not now. Not for me. But it isn't impossible, darling. And it might be necessary for me one day."

He drank from his glass and watched her pull the stole from her shoulders. She bent forward, her breasts swung out and she placed her hands on his cheeks. "You might like me better if I were in love with you, darling. The whole thing might make more sense."

"It might," he agreed.

She kissed his forehead slowly. "Thanks for the party, Web. You can get back to your writing now." She stood up, walked away from him and picked up her dress from the floor. "I should have phoned to find out if you were busy, and I'm sorry for the nonsense I talked."

"Oh, hell," he said. "Forget it."

She pulled the dress down over her head, took a compact out of her handbag and restored her lipstick. Then she combed her hair, put the comb back into her bag, and looked at Webster. "I hope you'll write well tonight. You ought to be relaxed."

"I'm relaxed."

"Who was the famous man who did his best writing right after he'd been with his wife? He was English, I think."

"William Blake," Webster said. "That who you mean?"

She nodded. "He was a poet, wasn't he?"

"Yes. He was a poet." Webster got up from the sofa and walked to Hildreth. He put his arms around her, and said, "If I don't see you before you leave, I'll come wherever you want."

Her face relaxed. "I'll wire you, darling. We'll have a wonderful time." She kissed him lingeringly and walked with quick steps to the door. She adjusted the stole around her shoulders, blew him a kiss and opened the door.

Webster watched the door close behind her, and when he could no longer hear her steps on the stairs, he went back to the typewriter, turned on the light and lighted a cigarette. He reread the page he had been working on and then he finished his drink. He was not relaxed, but tense, and he had to force himself to sit at the typewriter while he tried to remember what he had been about to write when Hildreth came. But in a little while he knew that it was gone, and he pulled the half-typed sheet from the typewriter and tore it up.

3.

In the late afternoon Robert Webster shaved and put on a clean shirt, mailed some letters and rode the *Metro* to the Abbesses stop. He wondered what it would be like at Lydia's and whether Tay would be there. He thought, I should have married someone like Hil instead of Alice Lee Crandall. She took the heart out of me with her childish idea of love and the way she resented every time I had to write. She must have thought the studios were paying me just to live in Bel Air as a public relations symbol. She couldn't understand that I had to have time to myself; time alone so that I could think and create. In a way she was ashamed because I wasn't a lawyer or a banker or something that her crowd was familiar with. To them I was a freak because I was a writer; a guy who made motion pictures. In their book I was like an acrobat or a magician and that was one of the things that destroyed us—if we ever had anything strong enough to be destroyed.

He took a taxi up the Butte to the Place du Tertre and climbed to the top floor of an old building that overlooked the city.

Lydia opened the door, and said, "So nice to see you, Robert." She shook hands with him and closed the door. Her atelier was two stories high with a broad ceiling skylight that faced the city. From a window he could see the white aloofness of Sacré-Coeur, its dome coraled a little in the afternoon sun.

Lydia wore old flannel trousers and a paint-stained artist's smock. An easel held a half-finished still-life. There was the smell of turpentine and paint in the atelier. She offered Webster a Camel and took one for herself. When Webster had lighted her cigarette, she said, "Sit down, won't you? You haven't changed as much as I would have thought."

"You haven't changed at all."

She pushed one hand through her bobbed, gray hair. "I'm trying not to feel my age. Is that a sinful aspiration?"

"Not at all. Do you like it here?"

"I tell myself I do. You can't imagine how dreary Pasadena became when my husband died and Tay was in New York. I felt as though my house had suddenly fallen apart, so I thought I'd spend my last few years in Paris." She looked sadly at Webster. "Now I know I should have spent my youth here."

"Paris isn't the same to everyone. I suppose you feel that by now."

She nodded slowly. "What has it been to you, Robert?"

"It hasn't been everything I thought it would be."

"You came here on business, I believe."

"Yes." He told her about the picture and Kress and Gringold.

"Bad luck," Lydia said. "Very bad luck, Robert. Now what will you do?"

"Try to do a good picture."

Lydia pointed to a tray of liquor bottles and glasses. "Make something for yourself. Unless you'd really like tea. I'll have a Martini."

Webster made the Martini carefully, using English gin and French vermouth. He made himself a Scotch and soda.

"I didn't think you'd be strong for hors d'oeuvres," Lydia said. "That's why there aren't any."

"I'm not. I haven't had good Scotch in a long time."

"You made very good money at the studios. Weren't you able to save any of it?"

Webster shook his head. "Not very much. And I was married to a woman who had been brought up with expensive tastes."

"Lee could never economize. By the way, you knew she married again?"

"No."

"Two years ago. Her husband's a rather mysterious figure to us. He's a Belgian diplomat Lee met in Washington. We hardly ever hear from her any more."

They drank for a while, until Lydia got up and went to a painting on the wall. She threw back the drape that had covered it, and said, "I painted Tay last month. It's not very good, but you may find the Crandall resemblance."

Webster walked to the painting and looked at it. "I do," he said. "She's very attractive."

"Tay's turned out rather well on the whole. She's getting away from the influence of her mother who is the terror of the Pasadena School Board, and Bennington wasn't particularly beneficial, but Tay won't make too many mistakes." She turned to Webster. "She's joining us for tea."

Webster nodded. "I remember her as just a girl."

Lydia dropped the drape over the face of the painting and sat down in her chair. "New York matured her a good deal. She's much more adult than Lee. Tay is very dear to me. She's everything Lee could have been and was not."

Webster said, "You told Lee that marrying me would be a mistake."

"I told her that not because I disapproved of you, Robert, but because I knew Lee very well. She needed to be constantly petted and babied and you simply didn't have the time. Isn't that so?"

Webster went over to the drink tray and warmed his highball from the bottle. "I'm glad Lee got over it."

"Did you?"

"Yes," he said. "It was a mistake, and you like to forget mistakes as soon as you can. I tried to keep the damage confined."

She held out her empty Martini glass and Webster filled it from the shaker. She said, "I thought alone you might have done more with your life."

"The motion picture industry sort of fell apart," Webster said. "With the cutback I stopped working. It's been that way for quite a while."

"Are you in love with anyone?"

"Not now."

"It might be good for you, Robert."

"It would carry responsibilities that I don't want and can't face. I've got to get myself straightened out."

"Do you have a mistress?"

"You could call her that. I don't support her."

"Is she married?"

Webster nodded.

Lydia stood up and walked over to the windows that faced the city. "I *am* glad I came to Paris, Robert. But now and then I become lonely. It's the fate of an old woman."

"You never liked many people."

"I may have been overly discriminating. I've learned that when close friends die or move away there's no one left. Not even friends-once-removed. My son and his wife were little enough company, God knows. They're civic-minded people with clubs and committees and Leagues and getting out the vote. This sort of thing was never my strong point; perhaps because California was a different sort of place when I was young. One went there to make money, then relax and enjoy the spending of it. Tay's parents have plenty of money, but they don't seem to enjoy it particularly. They've acted as though it were a burden."

"It never was to me."

"But you never really had that kind of money, Robert. You averaged a thousand dollars a week while you were working; not two thousand every week of the year with eight or nine hundred thousand in good oil securities and grain futures. You weren't a peasant, but you weren't one of the big rich. Did you ever have a yacht?"

"Not even a rowboat," Webster said. He looked out of the window at Montmartre below, and in the distance the rows of trees that marked boulevards and the curving embankments of the Seine. Smoke from factories hung low over the city. It was a time of day he liked.

Lydia said, "Tay found this place for me. Didn't she choose well?"

"Very well."

"I watch the sunset every evening through this window. The skylight lets me paint all day, but when evening comes, it's time to stop painting, anyway." Lydia paused, and said, "I'm a great-grandmother now."

"It doesn't seem possible."

She left him and went into another room and brought back a leather picture frame. She showed Webster the photograph of a blond baby with large eyes and a small nose. Webster nodded and gave her back the photograph. It was strange to see a child born to another man by the woman who was once your wife.

"What's his name?" Webster asked.

"Johnny."

The door of the studio opened and a girl came in. She took off her hat and walked to Lydia. Then she bent down and kissed her. She came to Webster, holding out her hand, and said, "Hello, Web. It's nice to see you."

"Hello, Tay. How've you been?" She was more beautiful than Lee. Her nose was smaller and she held herself more erect. Her hair was the same shade of chestnut that he remembered and her eyes were dark.

Lydia said, "You're unforgiveably late, darling. There are practically no Martinis left."

Tay made a face. "I'm not very fond of Martinis."

"Robert makes an excellent Martini. He might make a fresh one for you."

Tay lighted a cigarette while Webster made another shaker of Martinis. She said, "I got tied up in the office again; couldn't seem to break away." To Webster she said, "I won the *"Prix de Paris."* It gives me a year with *Madame.* If I'm lucky they'll keep me."

"I'm sure they will," he said, and poured her Martini.

"I'd love to stay on in Paris, wouldn't you?"

"I'll have to. Until the picture I made is distributed."

"Do you? I didn't think writers had anything to do with that part of it."

"Unless they've invested in the picture they don't. I made that mistake."

"If it's like your other pictures, Web, it will be really good."

"It isn't anything like my others."

Tay sipped her Martini and sat down on the arm of a chair. "I always thought you were still working in Hollywood."

"Not any more," Webster said. "It's a set for a ghost town with Gary Cooper striding down the main street looking for badmen."

Lydia said to Tay, "I'm glad you didn't bring Maude with you."

"Of course I wouldn't. You don't like her.

To Webster, Lydia said, "She's a tall, willowy creature in Tay's office who takes dope."

"Grandmother, I've told you Maude's a diabetic."

Lydia snorted. "Don't tell me, child. She's got an addict's waxy skin. She jabs herself all day long."

"She doesn't eat the right things. She needs vitamins."

"She needs six months of cold packs and forced feeding. You watch out for Maude. People like her always try to get their friends started. Besides, she looks like a Lesbian."

Tay colored. "Well, she's a little that way. She's not pretty enough to be attractive to men."

"Faute de mieux," Lydia said. "Well, you stay away from her. And don't let her give you any of her insulin."

"Of course not."

Lydia said, "Robert, Tay is really the nicest of all the Crandalls. She's much more intelligent than anyone elese in the family. Much brighter than her mother."

"Stop picking on Mother."

"I warned your father about her the first time I saw her. She really isn't very bright, dear, but none of her own family is."

Tay exhaled cigarette smoke and pointed toward the painting on the easel. "It's coming along well, isn't it? That's a very pretty blue."

"I'm glad you think so. In a few months I'll want to try another portrait of you. I might do Robert, too. After all, he belongs in the family gallery."

Webster smiled. "Only as a matter of history."

Lydia looked through the window at the illuminated basilique of Sacré-Coeur and decided that she ought to paint it before there was only gray winter lighting.

For an hour they talked of people they had known in Pasadena and Beverly Hills and Santa Barbara, and then Lydia said, "If I'd thought to buy a few things we could all have dinner here, but I'm dieting, you know. No sugar or fats."

Webster said, "We could go. over to the Cou-Cou for dinner," and looked toward Tay.

Tay said, "I'd like to."

Lydia shook her head. "I wouldn't be able to stay on my diet. I've got some consomme and skimmed milk here for myself. You two go wherever you want."

Webster finished his drink and saw Tay stand up. She smoothed the skirt across her thigh with her hands. Then she kissed her grandmother on the cheek. Lydia said, "Robert, if you have a little time tomorrow I'd like to do a few sketches of you. It would only take half an hour."

"When do you want me to come?"

"About four," she said, "if it wouldn't be too much trouble."

"Not at all."

Tay said, "She'll keep you here for hours. I thought she'd never finish my portrait."

"I'll come at four," Webster said. He shook hands with Lydia and followed Tay out of the door.

When they had gone Lydia locked the door and turned out the ceiling light. The studio did not darken completely because of the lights from Montmartre and the city beyond. Standing at the window she looked toward Sacré-Coeur again, and thought, I really ought to begin painting it tomorrow. If it's a nice day the light will be just right. In the winter it will be gray and there'll always be fog around it. I really ought to start tomorrow in the morning.

In a taxi, Tay Crandall said, "You know about Lee, don't you?"

"Yes."

"She was getting awfully bitchy just before she got married again."

"I can imagine."

"I was living in New York then, so I don't really know. It's just family talk."

"How was New York?"

She shrugged. "You've lived there, Web. You know how it is."

"Weren't you happy there?"

"Not very. It was a disorganized sort of life. I was at an ad agency then, and you know what that's like."

"I'm surprised you aren't married."

"Practically everyone else I knew got married; maybe that's why I didn't. It seemed the easy thing to do."

"No love affair?"

She nodded slowly. "Except that it was mostly too much drinking and hangovers and not liking myself very well." She turned to look at him, and said, "You aren't in love with Lee any more, are you?"

"Not any more. Not after so long."

She said, "What happened between you, Web? What went wrong?"

He lighted a cigarette, and said, "You know Lee; she couldn't share anything—not even marriage. When she couldn't fit herself into the requirements of my life she got out. I'm glad she did."

"Really?"

"Why not?"

"Oh," she said, "pride, I suppose."

He laughed a little. "There was no question of pride. And we didn't have any bedroom problems."

"I know you didn't. Lee told me you were pretty competent that way."

He looked at her in surprise. "Is that a usual topic of conversation between sisters?"

"Between us it was. And I was young and curious about those things. You see, you and Lee were a projection of the romance I planned to have. You were a hero of mine, Web. My first."

"By now you ought to be able to choose heroes a little more wisely."

The taxi slowed and stopped in front of the Hotel Crillon. They got out and walked into the bar. As the waiter showed them to a table, she said, "You didn't have much choice about this, did you, Web?"

"It's an excellent idea."

"Yes. Are you sure Lydia didn't suggest you sort of look out for me so long as we're both in Paris?"

"No."

He ordered a split of champagne from the waiter and a package of Luckies. Then he asked, "What do you do for *Madame?*"

"Fashion writing. It's a pretty specialized field; on the esoteric side. And I do a few sketches, too."

He smiled, "How does it feel to be grown-up, have a job, and an apartment in Paris?"

"I love being here. Have you seen much of France?"

"Not yet, but next week I'm going down to the Côte."

"I'm going there next month. For the *Rallye.*"

"Oh."

"It's a race from Menton to Cannes. I've never seen it before."

"Neither have I."

She said, "I can't imagine why your picture wouldn't be a good one. I still remember *Autumn Leaves.* You got an Oscar for that one. And there were so many other fine ones."

"I used to have producers who didn't assassinate my stories. The pair who got me to come here are a couple of amateurs, who can't tell a screenplay from a scratch sheet. Then I found out they owe money all over Hollywood. They owe me still for writing the picture, plus the money I invested in it."

"You'll get it all, won't you?"

"I suppose so. Eventually."

Two waiters went to a table and began helping a drunk toward the door. Tay glanced at them, and said, "How much of an evening are we going to have?"

"Some steaks and wine and dancing, if you'd like."

"Very much."

"There's a restaurant across the street called 'Yvonne et André.'"

She nodded, and after a while Webster paid the check and they walked across the rue Boissy d'Anglas and opened the carved wooden door that opened into the restaurant.

They dined at a table on the second floor, and the steaks were thick and blue at the center, and when they had finished a bottle of Beaujolais, Webster saw that the time was eight-thirty.

They walked around the corner of the American Embassy and crossed to the rue de Rivoli and there was mist in the air that formed a haze around the streetlights. In the Place de la Concorde the Obelisk was a tall pylon that rose high above the silver panaches of the illuminated fountains. The shop windows were lighted along the rue de Rivoli, and they looked at the displays of cheap tourist junk: printed scarves, metal models of the Eiffel Tower, ash trays, perfume flagons moulded into women's shoes and books with suggestive titles.

Across from them was the Louvre, its windows dark, and Tay said, "You've been there, haven't you?"

"The first week I was here."

"There's a modern art show down at the Trocadero."

"I've been there, too."

She laughed. "Why Web. I had no idea you were so interested in culture."

"I was interested in inexpensive entertainment."

"Where will be go to dance?"

'There's a place over near the Place Blanche called the Café Florence."

"I've been there," Tay said. "It's quite expensive. We could go some other place."

"Hell, I'm not broke. I've just been careful about spending until I could see more money coming in."

From the Place Vendôme they took a taxi up toward Montmartre and got out at the Café Florence.

For the Florence it was early and so far there were only a few other couples. Webster ordered a bottle of champagne and when the orchestra began to play he asked Tay to dance.

On the floor, she said, "It's been a long time since we danced."

"I know."

"I can even remember when it was. You and Lee gave a party in your garden and you let me come and bring a boy. You were nice enough to dance with me." She looked up at him and said, "I'm a better dancer now, and you're as good as you always were."

"It isn't something you forget."

"No." He could feel her moving easily against him, and he said, "You're the prettiest girl here tonight."

She put her cheek against his shoulder, and said, "Lee must have loved you more than you ever loved her. You knew so many attractive women then, even some motion picture stars, that I never quite understood why you married Lee."

"I thought she was different," Webster said. "She wasn't an ex-car-hop turned leading lady, she was from a Pasadena family and she was beautiful, and how can you tell how those things happen?"

"You can't."

When the music ended, they went back to the table and the waiter filled their glasses again. They drank for awhile, watching people arrive in evening clothes; all of them with money, Webster thought, except possibly the women. He looked at Tay, at the lines of her face and her lips, and he thought, I should have seen her before I saw Lee and I should have waited for her, but my luck's never like that. Either I don't wait long enough for something or I wait too long.

Now Lee was between them and in a way, Hildreth Kaufman. He knew that he could give up Hil if it came to a choice.

She said, "This is supposed to be a gay evening, Web. You shouldn't frown like that."

"Sorry."

"Is it something you'd tell me about?"

"It took a long time and Paris to bring us together."

"Yes."

Then they danced again, and in his arms she seemed more relaxed than before, as though she had made up her mind that there was no reason, now, why she should not be there, and finally, when the music ended, he added, "I wish I'd known before that you were living here."

"So do I," she said. "It could have made a difference."

And to me, he thought. He wondered where Hil was tonight; if she had gone to Spain or to the Côte, and when he would hear from her. He wondered whether he would go to her when she told him where she was. He knew that in the last few weeks he had been drifting closer to Hildreth Kaufman and that he had even begun to think of her in a way that would possibly mean a divorce from Frederic. But he knew that he had relatively little to offer her or any other woman. He was under forty, reasonably good-looking and sexually accomplished, but until he was making worthwhile money again, it would be hard to support a wife like Hildreth. Hil was used to more luxuries than even Lee, and so he would have to make more money than he had ever made. Still, Hil was better in bed than Lee had been; much better; and that side of it would be worth the extra effort.

But as they talked, he forgot about Hildreth Kaufman, and listened to Tay. Her voice was low and she had a quick, compelling smile. She could be serious and gay, and when she spoke to him he did not want to interrupt; he wanted her to say more. When she was in his arms on the dance floor he felt self-conscious and a little awkward—as though it were his first date with a girl.

When they left the Florence it was after midnight, and the champagne had come to more than six thousand francs, which was what his food had been costing him for a week.

They took a taxi to the rue St. Benoît near the Place St. Germain-des-Près. They got out in front of the door of a *caveau* that had begun after the war as an Existentialist cellar, and was now a kind of club that attracted a certain amount of tourist trade.

The door was tall and broad; oak studded with iron, and when he knocked, a porthole opened, and a man looked out and asked him for his card. Webster handed the man a hundred francs and the door opened.

4.

THEY WALKED DOWN THE CURVING STAIRS into the dimness of the *caveau*. Through the screen of smoke he could hardly see the walls and their schizoid paintings. There were angles and straight lines; strokes that waved like a kris and blobs of color in chartreuse, violet, green and brown. Imagination, fancy and compulsion had run free on the walls and the total effect was drugged illusion.

The cellar was jammed with people, sitting and standing. There was a motion of a kind, voices and laughter, and the air was very bad.

When he saw a vacant table, he pushed through a mass of people and they sat down. At the end of the cellar seven Negroes climbed up on the low bandstand and picked up their instruments. Webster wondered if they were American, French or Moroccan. He had heard that deserters from the "Red Ball Express" had hidden in Paris until the end of the war and melted into the Parisian population as black-marketers, pimps and musicians. These Negroes readying their instruments to play could have worn khaki once and rolled gasoline to the tanks of the Second Armored as it drove eastward to Paris and beyond.

He caught the arm of a waiter and ordered *fines à l'eau* as the band began to play. From the first chords and the offbeat rhythm he knew the music was as surrealist as the murals. The three saxophones sang blaringly high in unison, working around a weird pentatonic progression, answering back to the intermittent rhythm, and above them a derbied trumpet blared a challenge into the packed cellar. People began to dance slowly, moving like cogs compressed inside a circling wheel that rotated them in a tight pattern.

The music was tremendously loud, thrusting its aggressive cacophany through the cellar, stifling the air with its volume, smothering voices and laughter.

Tay said, "Much as I like dancing with you, I don't think it would be possible here."

"No. We're here for atmosphere; that's all."

As his eyes became accustomed to the dimness he could make out nearby figures. Beside him a couple kissed, their eyes closed, their bodies pressed closely together. The man was young and unshaven and he wore a sweater and a pair of dirty khaki trousers. Webster could not see the girl's face. In the *caveau,* wartime chino trousers and sweaters were almost a uniform and the men wore Army shoes or moccasins.

The *fines* arrived, brought by a sweating waiter, red-faced from pushing his way from the bar to the table. The cognac was so bad Webster decided it had been distilled in Portugal. He lighted Tay's cigarette and watched the musicians on the bandstand, seeing only their heads and shoulders above the huddled dancers. Two saxophonists were standing, taking four-measure solos in answer to each other. They played with their eyes closed, their fingers lifting and falling exaggeratedly against the keys. Their phrases drove on relentlessly in odd, dissonant intervals that gave the effect of playing in a different key from the others, and when the number ended he felt that it was not complete.

Off key and incomplete, Webster thought, as he watched the crowd move from the small dance floor and disperse among the tables. That's how the war left us.

Most of the faces he could see were younger than he was, and more than half of them looked American. Many of the girls wore horn-rimmed glasses that accentuated their close-cropped hair. Some of the men wore khaki shirts with Army or Air Force patches, and he realized that the *caveau* was a focus of Sorbonne and Université students whose tuitions were paid by the G.I. Bill.

Tay said, "I've heard of these *caveaux* before, but I've never been in one."

"I thought it might be a change for you."

"It's *quite* a change. Do you come here often?"

He shook his head. "Only when I need a few laughs."

A hidden spotlight went on, illuminating a microphone in the center of the dance floor, and the crowd began to applaud for someone who was apparently a favorite. Webster watched cigarette smoke curl upward through the beam of light like the smoke of distant fires on a still evening. From a door beside the bandstand a woman was walking toward the microphone and the applause grew loud and unrestrained. Her skin was café au lait and she wore a skin-tight, red velvet dress that pushed her large breasts together. Smiling, she bowed low, waving to the crowd, and then she turned to the band and nodded. The *caveau* became very still, and as the band began her introduction the singer stepped close to the microphone and touched it lightly with her hands.

She sang softly, without effort, her lips unsheathing white teeth, and her hands moulded her body to emphasize the faintly-accented words.

"Already it may be too late,
So, darling, don't hesitate..."

A sigh went through the crowd.

"Whether it's fair weather
Or if there comes a storm..."

Beside Webster a man whispered to his girl, "Isn't she *marvelous?* There isn't *anyone* like her."

"No," the girl agreed. "There's no one like her."

"... *The way your love goes*
Depends on how the wind blows..."

Then, in a little while, the song was finished, and the singer stepped away from the microphone to acknowledge the crowd's sustained applause. As an encore she sang in French and the words were suggestive enough to evoke whistles and wolf-calls from the men who understood the argot.

Tay said, "Do you like her?"

"She's no Lena Horne."

"No. Or Josephine Baker."

"You've been to her place, haven't you?"

Tay nodded. "Hasn't everyone?"

It came to Webster that only a few of the crowd would ever have heard of Josephine Baker and even fewer would have seen her perform. Shake your bottom, Josephine, men yelled the last time Webster had seen her, and Josephine had shaken her bottom. Of such stuff were entertainers made. But Josephine would never be found in this cellar of sweatered devotees whose incomes derived from the G.I. Bill. When Webster thought of her he thought of the Windsors, the Aga Khan, Eden Roc and Aix-les-Bains; of money that was endless and a world that had not survived the war and the clawing of the levellers.

He hardly noticed when the singer ended her song because the band took up its chase at the height of the crowd's applause, and before the floor filled with dancers a tall young man wth a crew cut led the singer from the microphone to his table and the spotlight went out. Tay stood up, and said, "If I can find it I'll be back in a minute."

He stood up, and noticed that their table had become a hub of moving bodies and the air was much worse than when they had come into the cellar. Tay's chair grated as someone moved against it, and when he looked up, he saw a girl glance down at him. She smiled quickly, turned toward him, and pulled the chair the rest of the way from the table. Then she sat down, put her elbows on the table and stared at Webster.

"Hello," she said.

"Hello."

"Aren't you going to buy me a drink?"

"Why should I?"

"Because you're an American. Probably an American tourist. Don't you want to buy a drink for a girl in a Left Bank *caveau so* you can tell the Lions Club about it when you get back to Kansas City?" Her face was placid. Her hair was drawn tightly back from her forehead and caught in a pony-tail behind.

"Try someone else," Webster said. "I live here."

Her eyebrows went up in surprise. "I don't believe you."

Webster laughed. "Why should I bother to lie to you? You're just another bad-mannered American girl in Paris. Smart but sloppy. And overdue for a bath."

The girl said, "I bathed myself this morning."

"In a *bidet?*"

The girl's face reddened. "You win. You looked like another Babbitt to me. I make a practice of baiting them. You don't have to buy me a drink. If you want to talk for a while, I'll buy myself one."

"Oh, hell, I'll buy a drink. If the waiter ever comes."

"What are you doing in Paris?"

"I came here to join the Foreign Legion," Webster said, "but I had the Old Joe so I got turned down. What are you doing here?"

"I don't think you've got whatever the Old Joe is," the girl said. She took a handkerchief from her sleeve and blew her nose. "I'm at the Université."

"Learning anything?"

"Of course I am. I wouldn't stay if I weren't." Her voice was angry.

"You'd stay if the place burned down. Does your mother know you're out tonight?"

"My mother hasn't anything to do with me. She lives in the States."

"Where?"

"Denver. Denver, Colorado."

"Don't feel ashamed of it," Webster said. "Everyone can't be born in France." He caught the waiter's eye and ordered two more *fines.* "What happened to your date?"

The girl shrugged. "He only brings me here. Then he always goes home with Gaby."

"Who's Gaby?"

"The singer. My God, she's the most sensational thing on the *Rive Gauche.*"

"The coon-girl in red velvet?"

The girl's face grew hostile. "Why do you call her a coon?"

"Because she's got tiny paws and she washes herself so clean."

"You meant it in a racist way."

"I meant it the usual way," Webster said. "Are you another Peace Fighter? Circulated any petitions lately?"

"I'm not an activist," the girl told him. "Not yet."

The waiter brought the *fines* and the girl raised hers to her lips. "Death to the status quo," she said, solemnly.

"To the guillotine with international bankers and cannibal war-mongers," he said pleasantly. "I'm surprised you don't feel self-conscious here tonight. In these surroundings, and having had a bath this morning, you could pass for a member of the bourgeoisie."

"I've identified my life with the struggle of the working class," the girl said, doggedly. "Even so, I believe I'm entitled to a little relaxation."

"Everyone is. And you can be confident that the monolithic unity of the peace-hungry peoples won't deteriorate while you relax."

"Well," the girl said, "you're really a typical reactionary, aren't you?"

"Racist. Racist reactionary. See, I know the phrases. Semantics are quite a thing, but I'm sure they aren't part of your studies."

"Why are you sure?"

"Because you've fallen for the double-talk of the times."

"You think that peace is only double-talk?"

"When you say peace and mean war it's double-talk," Webster said.

The girl finished the *fine* he had bought her, and stood up.

"You're beneath contempt. The peoples of the world want peace but you want war because your society has to have war to make its profits."

"See you at the barricades," Webster said. "Don't drink any Molotov cocktails."

The girl left his table, pushing her way through the crowd toward the table where the young man who had brought her sat drinking with the singer called Gaby.

In a little while Tay came back, and said, "There was a queue. Sorry I was so long."

"I had company."

She sat down and looked at him. "Someone interesting?"

"It was a type," he said. "She's one-third of a triangle."

"Not an usual type."

"No."

She finished her cognac, and said, "It's not very late yet. We could go back to my place for a nightcap and you could play the piano."

"I haven't played in a long time."

"I thought you'd have a piano in your apartment."

"Where I live the only pianos are in saloons."

She said, "I remember how well you used to play. You always had a piano before."

"That was in Bel Air," he said. "I had everything I wanted then."

"Yes," she said, quietly. "I suppose you did."

She turned on a table light in her apartment, and said, "Can you see to play?"

He nodded.

"Coffee or Scotch?"

"Scotch. We can have coffee later."

He sat down at the piano and watched her while she brought Scotch and ice and Vittel into the living room. He said, "Won't the neighbors complain?"

She shook her head. "They haven't yet, and I've had some noisy parties." She brought a highball to him, and he said, "What would you like to hear, Tay?"

"Whatever you'd like to play." She lighted a cigarette for herself. "Just play as though you were alone."

Webster thought back to the songs that had been popular in the first years after the war; those would be the ones that would mean the most to her. Songs that could bring back memories to him were ten years older.

His fingers moved easily into a slow melody, and Tay was beside the piano, half-leaning against it, smoke from her cigarette partly veiling her face. As he played he saw that her eyes seemed to deepen and her face relaxed as though her thoughts were lost in the past, and to Webster her face was young and very beautiful. When the last phrase of the song ended he did not stop, but began to modulate into another, and said, "I wish you'd sing this one."

"Do I know it?"

"I think so. Remember *Don't Worry 'Bout Me?*"

She nodded, and as he resolved the modulation she began to sing the words, slowly and with meaning, and her voice was quiet and vibrant, and when the song ended, she looked down at him, and said, "I wasn't very good."

"You were fine. You've sung before."

"Not for years, really."

"The things we like to do we don't do often enough. Wouldn't you rather sing than write for *Madame?*"

"Of course. Most of my writing talent went into pamphlets for the Socialist Party. I worked nights for them my first year in New York." She drank from her glass. "In my case socialism was something I grew out of; like football games."

She looked down at him and said, "I think I'd rather listen to you play than hear myself talk, Web. Schoolgirl confessions can't have much interest for you."

"They happen to," he said. "I remember you as you were, and now I see you as you are. I'd like to learn about the time in-between."

"Please play," she said. "We'll have other times to talk."

"Yes," he said, and began to play for her. He played *Laura* and *September Song* and *Autumn In New York,* and for Webster it was as though he was hearing them for the first time, and the melodies pleased him and quietness of the room and the look on the face of the girl.

When he stopped she took his glass, added ice and Scotch to it and a splash of Vittel. She brought it back to him, and said, "You're much better than the man I hire for parties."

"Thanks."

She tilted her highball a little, and then she said, "Tell me how often you've been in love."

"A couple of times."

"Then you've been lucky."

Yes, he thought, and it could probably happen again; now as I sit here looking at you. The atmosphere is right, because there's been dancing and music, and that's how people usually fall in love. It takes a background like that; it doesn't happen in the subway or a grocery store.

She moved closer to him, and said, "Because of who you were and because I was very young, I was a little in love with you, Web. Did you know it then?"

"No," he said, "but it's nice to know it now."

She said, "Being with you tonight is almost as though I were with someone I'd met for the first time." She hesitated for a moment. "Does that seem strange?"

He shook his head. Then he said, "You look a little like Lee, but otherwise you're nothing like her. I can't keep on thinking of you just as Lee's little sister."

"I don't want you to."

He said, "Our being brother and sister was something created around us artificially. But now you aren't just the sister of a woman I happened to marry a long time ago. You're someone in your own right." He touched his hands to the keys. "You're young and you're beautiful, and when I saw you this evening for what was really the first time, you brought something back into my life. Whatever it was, I'd been missing it for a long time."

"That's a nice thing to say, Web."

He drank from his glass again and replaced it on the piano. With his hands he struck a quiet chord, added bass notes, and began moulding the chords into a melody that had come into his mind. As he played he saw her come nearer to him and then he felt her hands on his shoulders. He looked up at her, but she said, "Please don't stop," and he saw that her eyes were closed and her lips were set. When the melody came to an end he reached up for her hands and drew her down next to him. He put his arms around her and her lips were trembling and open and very soft, and when he had kissed her for a long time he could feel her tears on his cheeks.

He said, "Tay, this is nothing to feel bad about."

She opened her eyes and looked at him. "It is for me," she said in a half-whisper. "I hadn't planned on anything like this. If you were still my brother-in-law this wouldn't have happened."

He kissed her again. He said, "Paris is a funny place. People do things they'd never think of back in the States. Six years ago you were a pretty young girl who was my wife's sister, and so far as I was concerned that made you untouchable. I hardly knew you existed. Now we run into each other and the situation's changed."

She put her hands behind his head and drew him down to meet her lips again. In his mind there was the music he had played and the mood it had created for them and the discovering of a desire that he was only beginning to understand.

After a while, she said, "I can't help thinking of Lee."

"I wish you could."

She said, quietly, "It's easier for you, but Lee's my sister." She stood up and moved away from him. "I don't want to remember her but I can't help it."

He stood up and drew her against him feeling her body comply without reserve.

Then: "I wish I didn't feel that way, Web."

"It isn't your fault."

"No. I didn't think it would be this way at all. There shouldn't be anything between us, Web."

"There could be," he said. "You know that, don't you?"

"I don't know." She ran her hand through her hair. "I guess you ought to go, Web."

"All right." He began walking toward the door.

"It was a wonderful evening. Really wonderful."

"I'm glad."

She walked toward him slowly, and said, "By now you'll have had enough of the Crandall tribe."

"We can't always live in Lee's shadow."

She shook her head slowly. "I haven't grown away from it yet. Maybe I never will."

"You will. Eventually."

"But you won't be here then."

"No," he said. "I won't be around."

She put her arms around his neck and said, "Just kiss me again, Web. Only once more."

"Yes."

Then: "Ah, Web, darling. No … if only I could."

"It's up to you."

"I want you. Really I do. It isn't that; you know what it is."

"It doesn't have to be."

"I know we've something between us now. Maybe there always was for me. We don't have to stop seeing each other."

"No."

"I wish I felt differently about it. Now. But it's too soon. It's come so quickly."

He opened the door, and said, "Good night, Tay."

"Good night."

He walked down the stairs to the Place des Saussaies. When he turned to look at her window he saw the light go out.

At Rond Point Webster took the *Metro* to the Odeon Station. Climbing up the steps to the Boulevard St. Germain he saw that it had begun to rain. He walked close to the buildings but he did not walk rapidly because he was remembering what had happened at Tay's apartment and how useless and unsuccessful the whole thing had been.

Near the Luxembourg Gardens he saw how the rain had wet the cobblestones in the street and turned them into polished ebony that glistened under the street-lights. His face and his hands were wet and he went into a *brasserie* for a cup of coffee before going back to his flat.

Sitting at the bar Webster asked for a *fine café*. He waited while fresh coffee was brewed in the big nickeled urn, noticing that another man was sitting at the bar eating hard-boiled eggs and drinking beer. The hard-boiled eggs were in a big, cut-glass bowl on the bar in front of the man who broke their shells, peeled them clean, salted them, and ate them pleasurably. When Webster's coffee came, he poured cognac into it and drank half the cup quickly to warm himself. The egg-eater turned to him and asked, "You American, too?"

"Yes."

The man pushed the bowl of eggs toward Webster. "Have an egg."

"No thanks."

"Go ahead. On me."

"Not now."

"Well, okay. Have a drink then."

"Thanks. I've got one."

The man slid the bowl of eggs back in front of himself, and pointed to a table in the corner. "Look at that. Four whores and a pimp. The guy comes over every ten minutes and tries to fix me up with one of them."

Webster saw that four whores and a pimp were at a round table in the corner of the *brasserie.* "They'll go away," he said.

"To hell with them." The egg-eating American cracked another egg on the edge of the glass bowl. "If it was four pimps and only one whore they might be able to twist me into it." He was a large man and his coat was tight around his shoulders. He was built like a hammer-thrower, and he had an amiable face that looked as though he had once done some boxing.

Webster said, "It's the way you eat eggs. The girls like the idea."

The man thought for a while, and then he said, "You may be right at that. But I don't eat them for any special reason; I just like eggs."

"Don't pay an attention and the pimp won't bother you."

"I don't even look at the girls but the pimp keeps coming over. Not that I got anything against them, but I don't feel like it tonight. You know how it gets to be."

Webster nodded.

"I came in here to get out of the rain, drink some beer and eat a few eggs, so the pimp wants me to charge out to a fleabag for a ten-minute roll with one of his dames, and I say the hell with it."

Webster saw the pimp look around at the egg-eater, and then he got up from the table and came over. He said something, and the American said, "For Christ's sake, no! How many times you have to be told?"

The pimp shrugged and put his hand on the egg-eater's sleeve, plucking at it gently. The egg-eater slapped the hand away. "To hell with you," he said. "I'm not bothering you and your dames; don't bother me." He turned away from the pimp and finished his glass of beer. The bartender drew another for him.

The pimp stood for a moment looking uncertainly at the American and then he wandered back to his table. The whores spoke excitedly to him, but the pimp shrugged and sat down. One of the whores took out a compact and powdered her nose. She looked at herself in the compact mirror, closed it and put it into her bag. She looked at the American and then she said something to the pimp. The pimp made a vulgar gesture with his hand.

The American said, "Why don't they throw them out? This is as bad as Memphis."

"Worse," Webster said. He finished his coffee and asked for another. The walk had tired him and he felt that he needed the coffee and cognac. At another corner of the room two old men played cribbage. They used matchsticks in place of cribbage pegs and they played very slowly.

When the coffee and the cognac began to work Webster began to feel better. He stirred the coffee and thought, for a while, of Tay Crandall.

After a while, the American said, "You like Paris?"

"It's all right."

"I like it okay. Trouble is, I don't speak the language. I guess you like a place better if you speak the language. I know the word for beer, the word for eggs and the word for whore, and that's all I know."

"That's all you need to know."

"You speak the language?"

"Pretty well," Webster said.

"Learn it in college?"

"Some of it. I've been living here for a while and that helps. When you've studied it once it comes back."

"Trouble with me is I never studied. I went to college, but I played ball all the time. They didn't bother me much about going to class."

"Have a good time?" Webster asked.

"Hell, yes. It was a little tough to keep training every fall, but the winters were okay until spring practice came around. I always had a job from some alumni in the summer. It wasn't bad. Plenty of quail," he said. "Young dames, you know." He lifted his beer and finished it. The bartender looked at him, but he shook his head. "I'm full," he said. "Damn good eggs. Cooks them just right. Must be fresh to start with."

Webster watched the ballplayer take some francs from his pocket and lay them on the bar. The bartender counted them and said, "More."

The ballplayer added fifty francs. The bartender held up his hand, scooped the francs off the bar and counted out some change. The pimp got up from his table and walked quickly over to the ballplayer. He began pleading with him, trying to pull him over toward the table. The ballplayer said, "For Christ's sake," disgustedly, and picked up the glass bowl of hard-boiled eggs. He pushed the pimp with one hand, staggering him backward across the floor to the table, and then he lifted the glass bowl into the air toward the table. It hit the top of the table, exploded and shot eggs onto the whores. Some of the eggs bounced off onto the floor. The ballplayer got down from his stool and watched the table. The whores were screaming, and the pimp had pulled a knife from his sleeve. He crouched low and began coming toward the ballplayer. The ballplayer laughed and turned, and then he ran quickly out of the *brasserie.* The pimp straightened up and began running, but as he passed, Webster tripped him. The pimp fell sprawling, the knife clattered across the stone floor and the whores screamed in unison. The bartender picked up the knife, quickly and hid it in his apron. The pimp got to his feet and came back slowly to Webster. He said, shakily, "Give me my knife so I can cut out his heart." The muscles of his face moved like worms under cloth.

"You don't want to try that. He'll pull off your head like a cabbage."

"Give me my knife," the pimp whined. His face was red and where he had fallen against it the skin was bruised and dirty.

"I haven't got your knife."

"You are lying; give it to me." He clenched his fist and Webster hit him. He landed backward against the edge of a table and his knees buckled. He tried to push himself at Webster again, but he could not make it. He fell forward and the whores screeched again. Two of them rushed to the pimp and began dragging him back toward the egg-littered table. They cursed Webster.

Webster took two hundred francs from his pocket and gave them to the bartender. The bartender said, "By itself the bowl is worth a hundred francs."

Webster gave him another hundred francs.

"*Merci,* m'sieu. I apologize for the unpleasantness."

"That comes from having whores around," Webster said.

"Sometimes there is only the choice of having them or having no one at all. When the weather turns cold they will be here most of the time."

In the corner the whores were sponging the pimp's bruised face. They chatted like monkeys and the bartender poured some cognac into a glass. He carried it over to the table.

The two old cribbage players had not paid any attention to the fighting and the broken glass. Webster watched the pimp begin to drink the cognac and then he walked out of the *brasserie*. In the street again, his hand began to hurt where it had struck the pimp's jaw.

The rain had stopped and the street was quiet, with only a few passing taxis, and most of the buildings were completely dark. Leaves and branches against the street-light made patterns of lace and filigree. The lights threw long shadows across the cobbles and the air was fresh and cool. He breathed deeply to clear his mind, and then he turned into the Boulevard Raspail.

5.

Sitting with a cigarette in his flat, he closed his eyes and realized that the only way he could stop thinking about Tay would be to go to sleep. He was stirred, still, from having been with her, and stimulated by the coffee in the café. Considering that he had only really met her that evening they had come remarkably close to understanding each other. He had not known anyone of her grace and beauty in a long time; not since Lee.

Now that they knew they liked each other there would be other times together when he could begin to assay exactly what there could be between them. It was something that would take time. Because he had one marriage fail, and with her sister, it was necessary to be even more sure of a second time.

He began to feel relaxed and satisfied from the evening, and he stretched his legs forward and leaned back against the sofa. The way he felt was as though he had just come back from the blinds when the mash before dawn had been white with drifting fog and you could hear flights of mallards skittering off the water and climbing invisibly into the black sky, their wings whirring like the ghosts of long-dead waterfowl. Then, seeing the swift passage of a flight across the face of the dying moon; hearing the air fill with restless, chuckling wings; searching the lightening sky until there was contrast enough to follow a moving target with your gun and fire. Then the tremendous rolling echo resounding to the base of the hills and back and the rush of thousands of frightened waterfowl into the sky. Later, under the sun, high vees of birds passing overhead that hesitated and wheeled at your call to glide downward toward your decoys, their wings set, their webbed feet trailing effortlessly, their bodies balancing the air currents, and when you were within range you led the barrel past the nearest one and fired, seeing the feathered body lurch with the pellets impact, the bowels empty themselves in a single jet of white before the wings locked against the body and the big drake fell twistingly into the water. You swung quickly onto the next, leading it until the set wings were spread toward you and the pellets broke them and that one fell downward after the other.

And afterward, when the limit was strung on thongs over your shoulder and you had rowed back to shore you walked to the cabin for a drink and in front of a fire your fingers became supple again and the liquor dissolved the fatigue that had come from crouching all day in the blind. The drinking was always better because you had killed cleanly and left no cripples in the reeds for snakes or falcons, and you knew that the next morning would be like the one that had ended.

Only that was too long ago to be recaptured, he thought, as he looked at the typewriter beside him, and the memory of it slipped away into the distance of his mind as he stood up and walked to his bedroom.

At four-thirty in the morning, Frances Thayer Crandall was wakened by the blare of an ambulance. She lay half-awake, listening to the sound of the ambulance recede into the night, but it had frightened her a little, and she could feel that her hands were clenched tensely and the muscles of her face were taut.

After Robert Webster had left she had made a drink to calm herself but now she knew that it had not done any good. He had made her want him, and the touch of his lips had been exciting because it had seemed, somehow, illicit. She sat up and turned on the bed light and opened a copy of *Deux Mondes*, thinking, if I read a little while I'll get sleepy again and I'll be able to sleep until morning. But if I don't, I'll lie here the rest of the night and think about Web and wonder about him and what happened to us this evening.

It wasn't only Lee between us; it was Rino, as well. But I couldn't tell him that; not without having him think I'm just another little trollop. Because I couldn't tell him, he won't understand and I'll never see him again.

I wonder if Lee ever felt the way he made me feel tonight with his arms and his body and his lips ... probably so, because they went all the way and didn't stop the way we did tonight. He wanted me, too, just the way I wanted him, but it wouldn't have been right if we'd gone ahead. Not so much because of Lee but because of Rino, even though I don't love him any more.

She closed the copy of *Deux Mondes* and put it back on her night table, thinking, I ought to turn out the light now and close my eyes and go back to sleep. It's nearly five now, and I have to get up at eight. I ought to do it, because if I don't I'll feel like hell. I'll look like hell, too. I'll look like Maude who never has a date with anyone except with me, occasionally, and I wonder if grandmother was right about her; the dope and being the kind she thinks Maude is. She can't help it if she's tall and bony and her skin isn't good. She might have a heart condition like those blue babies I saw once in the *crêche.* A bad valve in the heart does that, but they can operate now and cure it. They can cure the babies now, and I'll ask Maude if she has that kind of heart. That might be all that's wrong with her. That and diabetes, and the University of Toronto, or McGill.

I wish I could stop thinking about the blue babies. I shouldn't think about babies ever, because that's just what I don't want. Not now. Not ever, maybe. There are plenty of babies you can adopt. Here or in Switzerland or in Los Angeles. You don't have to have them yourself any more. It's much easier the other way. And I'd love it just as much; I know I would. I'd take care of it just as if it were my own, and I'd love it even more because it hadn't stretched me and made a cow of me, the way babies do when you have them.

She thought, it must be the time of the month again and that's why I'm thinking about babies. Only this month I'm sure. Really sure. Because we were never so long without it before. Never so long, so this month I don't have to worry.

But if Web were here right now I could forget about Lee and Rino and I'd let him. Yes. I know I would. And then if it were really good and something happened to me I could go to sleep afterward. I wouldn't worry about rhythm or those things Rino uses sometimes, we'd go ahead anyway because I'm so tired and I feel so really dreadful and I need sleep. Dear God, to be able to sleep all day tomorrow and not have to pull myself into the office and prop my arms on the drawing board and pretend to be the eager career girl they expect you to be. How simply wonderful to stay in bed all day and get enough sleep for once.

If I take a sleeping pill now I'll sleep right through the alarm and when I wake up I'll feel drugged and I'll put on stockings that don't match and my lipstick won't look right and altogether I'll be a mess. But it would be wonderful to take one. Just this once. And then sleep for eight hours.

She got out of bed, fitted her feet into her slippers and walked into the bathroom. She drank a glass of water and took the bottle of sleeping pills from the cabinet. Looking at the bottle she unscrewed the top and took one from it. Then she put the bottle back into the cabinet and filled the water glass again. She carried the pill and the glass to her bedroom and put them down on the night table. Then she kicked off her slippers and got back into bed. For a while she looked at the pill, thinking, even half of it would put me to sleep now. Just half of it would let me sleep for four hours. And I'd only feel half as bad when I woke up. And the alarm would still wake me.

If I drink a lot of black coffee as soon as I get up I'll feel all right and I'll be able to work and I won't feel so dreadful. I shouldn't try to have a job and go out all the time the way I do. I ought to do one thing or the other. That's why Maude's so good; she never goes out. All she does is stay in the office and work. And take her insulin. If it's really insulin, after all, and not what grandmother thinks it is.

I feel sorry for her, poor thing, because what she really ought to have is a love affair. Or even just an affair without the love. It might do her just as much good.

She took the pill from the night table and with her fingernail she made a line on it, dividing it, and broke it in two parts. It broke unevenly, and she put the larger part back on the night table. Then she sipped the water and swallowed the smaller part of the sleeping pill.

Turning off the bed light she lay back and pulled the covers over her body. Only four hours, she thought, that's all I can let myself sleep; and not even that much. I suppose Mohammedan women get to sleep all day long if they want to. In Saudi Arabia or Turkey or Iran or wherever they still have harems. If that's what grandmother meant about not being Mohammedan. Or did she mean the same man can't have two sisters? If that's what she meant I never knew it before, but for a woman her age she knows things I've never even heard of. I guess that's what it was. Like incest. If that's part of Mohammedan law it's actually based on sibling rivalry. A good reason for everything. Like not eating pork because of trichinosis. Except Web isn't one of the family any more and I've never eaten anything but well-cooked pork. So I haven't violated any laws at all. Only the ones that everyone else does.

Her eyes closed and she felt her body begin to relax, knowing that the drug was beginning to work. She smiled in the darkness because she had defeated fatigue and she would feel well when she woke. Really well. The way she felt now. And it was like letting yourself slip slowly into a warm depth that was without motion and the feel of the warmth coming up over your body in a sensuousness that was good in itself, and knowing that whenever you wanted to you could be submerged completely…

In the morning Robert Webster went out beyond St. Cloud to the studio projection room and watched while the picture he had made was run for him. When the lights went on again he stubbed out a cigarette and decided that it was possibly not as bad as he remembered it. Maybe the French would like it. He could get his investment back if it had a good showing in Europe, even without the export profit.

He worked in his flat for a while, scribbling in a notebook, writing down ideas as they came to him, and a little before four o'clock he took a taxi to the Place du Tertre.

Lydia was painting when he walked into the studio, and she turned, and said, "I'm sorry I'm still working, Robert. I didn't actually think you'd come."

He sat down and watched her dab at the canvas. "It was a date," he said.

"Yes, but people aren't often punctual nowadays." She laid down her brush, wiped her hands against her smock and took it off. Then she asked the cook to bring them ice.

Webster made a shaker of Martinis, and watched her start to sketch him. She used a piece of charcoal on a pad of drawing paper, and sipped her Martini as she worked. After a while, she said, "You don't have an easy face to work from."

"No."

"Anyone can draw a baby's face," she said, "but when a face is formed and mature it becomes difficult. Now, you have a strong face, Robert."

"So they say."

"It has a brooding quality to it that I want to capture if I can. I'm afraid it's going to take longer than I said."

"All right."

Finally she let him rest; and he said, "We had a good time last night."

"I thought you would. Tay's good company."

"She's an attractive girl."

"Isn't she, though! She's always liked you, Robert."

"I hardly knew she was alive."

She emptied her glass and held it out to him to fill. Then she said, "Tay makes people aware of her. She isn't to be ignored."

"No."

"Do you happen to be in love with her?"

He said, "I don't think so; not yet. We had a wonderful evening up to the time that Tay began to have qualms about Lee." He looked down at his drink. "I can understand how she might feel, but won't she get over that?"

Lydia put down her cigarette and leaned forward. She said, "Very likely. Unless Tay's following Mohammedan customs, her sister shouldn't be any issue at all. Tell me, Robert, did you spend the night with her?"

He looked at her, hardly believing he had heard her correctly. "That's a startling question for a grandmother to ask," he said. "As a matter of fact, I didn't."

Lydia picked up her cigarette, and sighed. "Then she must feel a sense of obligation to her lover."

He felt his body begin to chill. "She has a lover?" he asked.

"Oh, yes. For quite some time."

The stem of the glass felt odd to his numbing fingers. He put it down and looked at it. There was not much left of the drink. He said, "Couldn't you have stopped it?"

"Why should I? Tay's of age. She has her own life to live."

"Is a little guidance from you too much to expect?"

"Possibly not. But if I were to interpose any objection Tay would feel challenged to continue. I feel it's better this way."

"I don't," he said. "It's a lousy way to look at it."

"Tay means more to me than Lee ever did. I treasure even the little contact I have with her over here. I wouldn't jeopardize that for the sake of being a moralist." She looked at her cigarette holder, and said, "Does that shock you?"

"Yes, it does."

"I'm sorry, but that's how I'm approaching it. The man's name is Rino Menotti. He is handsome and presentable and wealthy enough to do nothing but drive his cars in races. He is married, and because he is Italian he will never leave his wife." She looked upward after some smoke she had exhaled. "Anyway, I don't think Tay is in love with him."

"Apparently the question never came up."

She said, "I was never consulted in the matter by either of them."

"Is she going to the Riviera with him?"

Lydia nodded.

He said, bitterly, "She could have told me. She didn't have to humiliate me."

"Do you think she is obligated to turn each date into a confessional?"

"This wasn't just another date."

She said, "Are you sure of that?"

"Yes." He stood up and looked at Lydia. "I'm sure of it the way you are, you're a pretty poor example for anyone. You've lost your self-respect and you talk more like an old procuress than a grandmother. If you had any love for her you'd have stopped it before. You'd stop it now."

She said, "You're being absurd."

"No."

"Yes, you are. You think because you suddenly meet her again that time ought to roll itself back to when you first knew her as a young girl. Well, Robert, in my opinion you're acting ridiculously. You're a sophisticated man of the world, but you're talking like a high-school boy."

"The hell with you," he said. "The hell with both of you."

"All right. If that's how you feel."

"That's how I feel. You're disgusting. Grandmother? Christ, you're only a smutty old woman living for second-hand thrills." He felt himself shaking as he walked away from her. "Lee brought me nothing but trouble and heartbreak. When I ended with her, I should have known it was all to the good. I don't want to see any of the Crandall tribe again."

As he walked out of the door she did not reply.

He went down onto the Place du Tertre, thinking, all right. Now I know about them. I know about Tay and her wop lover and the scab-picking old woman who doesn't want to grow old. To hell with the Crandalls. To hell with all of them. I shouldn't have come here yesterday, but I thought after six years it wouldn't matter. That shows how wrong you can be.

Well, he thought, I'll get over it, but I'll have her on my mind. For a long time. For as long as I'm in Paris.

He took a taxi to Roland's apartment near the Porte de Versailles. Roland's door was not locked and Webster walked in. He called, but when Roland did not answer, he made a drink in Roland's kitchen, brought it back to the piano and sat on the bench.

For a few minutes he played the piano but its out-of-tune dissonance made him stop, and when he had finished the drink he sat on a sofa and began reading a story in *Paris-Match* about the war in Indo-China. Then he made another drink and smoked one of Roland's cigarettes. Webster had almost decided to leave when he heard a key turning in the lock. The door opened and Roland came in.

"*Tiens, tiens,*" Roland said. "You are a magician that you come through a locked door?"

"You didn't lock it."

"Ah. Well, that may be so. I left in a rush when I was summoned to the presence of our former employers." He put his key into his pocket and picked up Webster's drink. He drank from the glass and revolved it between his fingers. "We have almost arrived at an accord."

Webster sat forward. "On another picture?"

Perrex nodded. "They say they will have sufficient funds within the month."

Webster shook his head. "I heard this might happen, but I didn't believe it."

"You heard, but you did not tell me? What species of friend are you?"

"I said I didn't believe it."

Roland gave Webster's drink back to him. "They want very much that you write a fine story for them to film."

Webster laughed shortly. "I only contribute once a year to Kress and Gringold."

"You have so much money that you can afford not to work?"

"I haven't been paid for the first time." Webster finished the rest of his drink. "If I have to work without getting paid I'd rather work for fellows I like."

"But you could insist that they pay you what they owe you before you begin the next work."

"All I want is three thousand dollars for writing the film, and eventually the five thousand I invested. Then they can get any writer they want."

Roland sat down beside Webster. "Believe me, I do not understand what has happened in their office, but I found them both most amiable." He took a cigar from his breast pocket. "Do you smoke cigars?"

"No."

"Neither do I." He laid it down on the table. "I will save it for some old woman who has the addiction." He looked at Webster. "Your only problem would be to write in a part especially for a lady who is to be in the film."

"That isn't impossible to do. Who's the lady?"

“I do not know. They spoke of her as Suzette.”

Webster sat back against the sofa. “She’s a friend of Frederic Kaufman’s.”

“Well, since you are a friend of Frederic’s wife you might find it amusing to write a part for a friend of Frederic.”

“The thought doesn’t amuse me,” Webster said. “Anyway I’m leaving Paris in a few days.”

“Oh? And where do you go?”

“South.”

“You will not go alone, of course?”

“Hildreth believes we need a change of scene.”

Roland smiled. “I understand perfectly and I approve. While I stay in Paris to work, in effect for the husband, you will be working on the Côte d’Azur with the wife.”

Roland lighted a cigarette and looked out of the window. “The Côte can be a place both dangerous and disappointing. When I was nineteen I went there with a woman who was a friend of my mother’s. She was a widow and she had been extremely kind to me. You understand?”

“I understand.”

“So, while we were staying at Cannes, she exercised her passion for walking and one lamentable afternoon she fell into a well that had been boarded over, but the boards were rotted away.” He shielded his face with one hand. “My friend, picture my descent into that ancient well to assist my mistress—the slimy rocks, the peril, the anguished screams of the wounded—it was an act of chivalry that I have never equalled. I bruised myself severely, but she had suffered a broken thigh, and I was obliged to become her nurse for nearly three weeks. Believe me, old bones knit slowly, and in her confinement she developed an ugly disposition, blaming me quite illogically for her tragedy. Long before she could be moved from Cannes we were snarling at each other like two hostile dogs, and the affection that had carried us there became only a thing of the past.” He looked at Webster’s smile. “You may think that I am not in earnest when I warn you against the perils of the Côte, my friend, but in all sincerity I urge you to limit your activity to the bedroom and the beach."

"That's the general intention," Webster said.

"You are definitely going away?"

"Yes."

"But you will talk with Paul and Henri?"

"If they call me. I'd want guarantees regarding payment and the integrity of the story."

"You are so right. They have treated you miserably. The approach must be theirs alone." He looked at his wristwatch, and got up from the sofa. "I must go to the studio to learn how soon production might begin. Will you go with me?"

"No." He stood up and followed Roland from the apartment.

Now, much later, in Montparnasse, Robert Webster was drinking beer at a sidewalk table of a *brasserie* on the Rue des Plantes. It was light Alsatian beer and it was very cold. It seemed to be making him sober. The Rue des Plantes was quiet, and in the last hour not more than five people had walked past his table. In that time the only unusual noise he had heard was the bray of a fire *klaxon* somewhere near the Seine.

The *brasserie* had a local family trade that drank inside the cafe part. On the sidewalk he was almost alone. His table was far enough away from the corner street-light that the light did not bother his eyes.

The waiter brought another glass of beer; it was even colder than the last. He said, *"Très froid,"* approvingly to the waiter.

The waiter bowed slightly, put his tray under his arm and went back into the lighted café. As Webster sipped the cold beer he watched the globe of the corner street-light. Half screened by branches and leaves it flickered like a galaxy of stars. So much for tonight, he thought. So much for Frances Thayer Crandall and faith and trust and love. I was wrong about her the way I've been wrong about so many others... only this time it hurts a little more. A hell of a lot more. Well, it's not fatal this time. It would have been a lot worse if I'd really fallen in love with her and then this had happened. Because it was always there to come up, and thank God it came out this afternoon. So now I'll have a month to write somewhere on the Côte, and she can go away with him wherever she wants and stay with him as long as she wants. Forever.

He began to remember again how it had been with her and the touch of her hands and her lips, but he forced it out of his mind, and called the waiter and paid the check. He walked away from the *brasserie* to the corner street-light, and saw that people were leaving the café. After a while its lights were turned off and the waiters left, locking the door behind them.

He saw a taxi standing at a corner a block away, and he began walking toward it. From the shadows of the street a woman came toward him. She was small and bareheaded and her shoes had high, spike heels. She began to walk beside him, and he saw that her face was young and rather pretty. She smiled, and said, "You 'ave one cigarette for me?"

He stopped to give it to her and she lighted it from a box of wax matches. She inhaled deeply and moved herself against him. She put her arms around his hips and rubbed her body against his. Her breasts were small and soft. She said, "It is ver' late, *mon ami.* You will go with me?"

"No."

"I could make you ver' happee."

"Not tonight," Webster said. He turned from her and began walking again, but the girl caught up with him and said, *"Je sais bien la mode Turque. Très bien.* You un'erstan'?" She made the gesture with her body.

"Not the way I feel."

The girl stopped smiling and pointed at his loins. "If you are sick there, I am ver' sorree."

Webster gave her fifty francs. "I'll have it taken care of."

"*Merci, m'sieu.* When you are well, come back *autrefois* an' ask for Simone." She folded the francs and pushed them into the top of her blouse.

Behind him he heard her call, *"Dormez bien, Americain,"* and when he reached the corner he looked back to see if she were still standing there, hands on her hips, legs apart. But she had moved back into the shadows and the sidewalk was empty.

In the taxi he rode with his eyes half-closed, thinking of Tay Crandall and the girl, whom, under other circumstances, he might have taken home with him.

6.

THE CONCIERGE BROUGHT HIM A MESSAGE in the morning from Paul Gringold, and when she had left he thought for a while about what Roland had said. Then he took the *Metro* to Rond Point and walked up the Champs-Élysées to the Cygne offices.

Hélène said, "They are expecting you, Monsieur Webster. You may go in." Her tone had lost its haughtiness.

Kress and Gringold sat behind their desks. Gringold wore a flowered Hollywood tie and Kress had a wing collar and a bow tie. They both stood up.

"Hello," Webster said. He walked to them and shook hands. The partners exchanged relieved glances.

"We've been tied up lately," Gringold said. "Working on the distribution, Web. You know how it is."

"Sure."

Kress cleared his throat. "We 'ave made much progress, Monsieur Robert. Only a few details remain."

"We're working on them now," Gringold said. "We expect to have everything sewed up by the end of the week.

Webster said nothing.

"Hélène did say that you 'ave come by one time." Kress took a check from his pocket and handed it to Webster. "A mistake was made, *mon ami*. My regrets. I 'ope that we are friends once more."

Webster folded the check without looking at it and put it into his billfold.

Gringold laughed nervously. "Henri must have been thinking of someone else when he sent you the other check."

"Of Hélène?" Webster asked. He turned and started to leave.

"One moment," Kress called, and the partners came from behind their desks. Gringold put his arm across Webster's shoulders. "Just a second, fellow. We've got some business to talk over with you. I think you'd like to hear about it."

Webster looked at his watch. "Will it take long?"

"No. No, it won't take long at all. Sit down, Web. Hell, we haven't had a talk in a long time. Too long."

Webster let himself be eased into a leather-covered chair. Gringold got out a cigar, creased the end of it with his thumbnail and lighted it. Finally, Kress said, "We are going to make another picture, Robert. Frederic Kaufman will back us. Perhaps you would like to do the story?"

Webster shook his head. "I'm busy until January."

Gringold's face fell. "Why didn't you tell us, Web?"

"You know how it is," Webster said. "Something comes along and you get preoccupied with it. Somehow I didn't think you'd be interested."

"Now, Web, we're still partners. Just because we had a few little misunderstandings at the studio last time doesn't mean we can't make good pictures together. One swallow doesn't make springtime."

"I'm leaving Paris in a few days. I need a vacation. I can't write well in Paris. It's too noisy... too many people." He stood up. "Maybe in the spring..."

Kress looked angrily at Gringold. "Monsieur Robert, you do not completely understand the position. Paul and I 'ave commited ourselves to make a picture by a certain date, but so far we do not 'ave a story from which to cast. We will 'ave the studio in three months. When we make the commitment we felt you would be able to write for us our story."

Webster shrugged. "You should have told me."

Gringold took the cigar from his mouth. "Look, Web, we're in a spot. You sign with us for another picture and we give you the other three thousand we owe you."

"The three thousand is part of a picture I've already done. I can't look on it as a bonus."

"I don't mean it that way. The point is, we'll have to go to a lot of trouble to get our hands on that much money right now. If we do, you ought to look at it like it was a gesture of good faith. A bona fide, you might say."

Webster shrugged. "We could call it that."

"You're only writing on spec for anyone else," Gringold said. "I'm talking about a cash on the drumhead deal."

"I'm writing an original for a studio that makes four pictures every month. How many do you make every month?"

Kress pushed past Gringold. "Please, Monsieur Robert. There is no reason we should be unpleasant. Another studio will change your story. We would let it be filmed exactly as you wrote it."

Webster laughed. "Like last time?" He shook his head. "Sorry, boys. I'm afraid I can't do anything for you." He started to walk toward the door again.

Gringold walked beside him. "How long will you be away, Web?"

"A month."

"Hell, you can do two stories in that time."

"You said something about a gesture of good will."

Kress said, defeatedly, "In two days you will 'ave the rest of the money we owe you. There, is that not a way to do business?"

"It's a good way," Webster said. "We should have done business that way before. If I get the money we'll talk about the new picture."

"Yeah," Gringold said. "I'll sell my blood to get your money for you. Two days—like Henri says—then we'll have a contract ready. In the meantime, start thinking of a solid bread-and-butter story revolving around the adventures of a *midinette*-type French girl."

"What does she look like?"

Gringold glanced at Kress. "Kind of German-looking I'd say. Blonde hair and pug nose. She don't look real French."

"Well," Webster said, "You can always dye her hair." He went out of the door, past Hélène, and into the hallway. He walked down the stairs, thinking, maybe I'll get my money after all. The money for writing the screenplay and even what I put into the picture.

If things were going to work out that way he would write a story outline while he was away with Hil. If Roland directed and the story was not changed by Paul and Henri it could have a chance for American distribution. Even with Frederic's mistress playing in it.

That's what I want, he said, half-aloud. I want a good picture to send back to the States, something that will bring back the prestige I used to have. It will only take one picture to do it. One good one.

When he walked past the *concierge's* lodging she came out to hand him a letter that had come by *pneumatique*. He opened it and saw that it was an invitation to a party the next evening. The party was being given by Tay. He saw that the letter had been mailed earlier that morning and then he tore it across and dropped it on the pavement. He thought, that makes her more cynical than I thought she could be. She'll have the wop there, of course, and what she wants is a chance to see us side by side and compare us. She can compare the way we look, the way we dress, the way we hold our liquor and she can even feel our muscles. But I'd be at too much of a disadvantage because I haven't slept with her.

He felt anger for her then, and for Lydia. He felt that they had deceived him, and he resented the way they had come back into his life.

On the day that Gringold had promised to send his money Webster was eating a lunch of cheese and fresh bread in his flat when Roland Perrex opened the door and came in. Webster offered a bottle of Danish beer to Perrex.

Perrex poured beer into a glass and sat in a chair.

"Cheese?" Webster asked.

Perrex shook his head.

"Bread?"

"Equally no. I have finished my lunch." He leaned forward and looked at Webster. "You saw *les macreaux,* did you not?" he asked.

"Yes."

"With what success? Tell me."

Webster told him.

Perrex turned down the corners of his mouth. "I do not think your money will come today."

"Why not?"

Perrex drank from his glass. He lowered it and looked at the head of foam. "I have just left the office. Not even Hélène was there."

"Probably they took Hélène to lunch."

"But I had an appointment. To discuss the rental of the studios."

Webster carried the bread and cheese to the kitchen. He wrapped the cheese in a damp cloth and put the cut loaf in a box. Then he went back to Perrex. "You think something may have happened to their plans?"

"Everything these two touch turns rancid." He stood up and smacked a fist into the other palm. "Does it not concern you?"

Webster sat down and finished his glass of beer. "I don't like the thought of not getting my money. Other than that, no. I've never wanted to write for them again."

"But I want to direct for them a second time. For you it is easy to be philosophic because you are a writer who can write books and stories and does not always need producers. But I am a film director, *mon ami,* and if I cannot persuade producers to make films then I am without work. To me their defection would be a tragedy."

"Have another beer."

"I would vomit it up. My God, Robert, how can you smile at this tragedy? I came to you for consolation, and you reject me completely."

"Not completely. I offered you a second beer. I offer it again."

Perrex's face relaxed a little. "One might as well be comfortable." He opened another bottle and poured beer slowly into his glass.

"What could have gone wrong?" Webster asked.

"Who knows? Perhaps Frederic's principals were struck with the unwisdom of his proposal. Because *he* is a fool is not reason to suppose that his principals are equally mad."

"It's a possibility. But as yet we have no contract with them. They may have found other employees."

Perrex groaned. "You will definitely rid me of my lunch. It was a good one, also; eaten in anticipation of employment, and therefore much better than usual. *Merde!* I urinate on their balding heads."

Webster said, "They could be lunching with the future distributors of our film. Don't read tragedy into an empty office. That's more symbolism than Cocteau."

Perrex shook his head. "I have ceased to understand you. If they neither pay you nor hire you to write their next film, what will you do?"

Webster picked up a telegram from the coffee table. "Go to Eze," he said.

"So? This Eze, where is it?"

"A few kilometers to the west of Monaco."

"Then I will pray that snow falls on the Côte as reprisal for your lack of charity to me."

"When I come back you ought to have everything ready to make a picture."

"I will have everything ready to become a bankrupt."

"You'll have a pair of producers, a studio and Suzette. What else will you need?"

"A story. Something at which to point the cameras. If you were a friend you would stay here writing, and not go to Eze. If you wrote an exceptional story we would not even have to take it to *les macreaux;* we would be able to choose our own producers."

Webster said, "I've let it worry me too long. To hell with Kress and Gringold and their problems. It's a waste of time."

"Only because you have a *patronne* who waits for you at Eze. My immediate prospects are less cheerful." He drank the rest of his beer. "You do not intend to see Paul and Henri again before you leave?"

"No."

"I admire your detachment, and I regret my inability to simulate it," he said a little stiffly. *"Bon voyage."*

Webster said, "Go back to their office and wait for them. At least there'll be Hélène to play with. You can pinch her behind." He lighted a cigarette, inhaled and looked out of the window. The midday sun reflected from the tops of trees along the Boulevard Raspail. Before eating his lunch he had almost resigned himself to not seeing Paul Gringold and getting his money.

To Perrex, he said, "In life one cannot lose every move. If we do not make another picture for Cygne, eventually we will make one for someone else."

"But in the meantime we starve."

"Nobody starves in France. Starvation in Paris is a bohemian fiction cultivated for the benefit of tourists."

Perrex said, sarcastically, "What magnificent detachment. *Alors!* You would have me apply to the *Syndicat d'initiatives* for employment as a tourist spectacle. Well. *mon vieux* at least it is a suggestion, and your first of the day. You have an enviable ability to solve the insoluble." He picked up his gloves, slapped them across one wrist, and said, "I give you joy of your Riviera interlude."

"If anything develops you might write."

"At Eze. *Très bien, alors. Au revoir.*"

Perrex went out of the door, closing it behind him, and Webster opened another bottle of beer. He took it to the window and looked down at the movement of traffic on the Boulevard below. The train to Nice did not leave until ten o'clock that night, so there was still time to hear from Cygne Productions.

Roland was suffering the results of being an enthusiast. He had counted on the word of Kress and Gringold, and made plans that depended on two men who had frustrated him once before. It would be good to have the three thousand dollars, Webster thought, but he would have it all in five more payments without being under any obligation to talk about writing another screenplay for Cygne. In five months he should be able to find other work. Better work.

When he finished the beer he looked at his watch and saw that the time was two-thirty. He felt drowsy, and after a while he fell asleep on his bed.

The *concierge* woke him at four o'clock to say that he was wanted on the telephone. On the landing below, he answered the phone and heard Gringold's voice.

"Web," Gringold said. "Things are held up at this end. I worked like hell but I still can't raise all your dough."

"How much did you get?"

Gringold coughed. "Only two thousand, Web. Jesus, you don't know what I had to go through to get even that much! The dough for the next picture ain't in our hands yet, so we'll just have to wait."

"Too bad."

"Yeah, tough. I knew you'd be a good sport. Say, how about having dinner with us tonight so's we can talk about the new story?"

"I'm leaving tonight."

"Look, put it off a day or so. We got to get this picture rolling."

Webster said, "I've made my plans, Paul. We made a bargain, but you didn't keep your part of it."

"I tried, Web. God almighty, how I tried. Don't that count for something?"

"It counts," Webster said, "but it's not what we agreed."

"You're putting the knife in me," Gringold groaned. "Take it out, Web. Be reasonable."

Webster laughed shortly. "Every day I worked for you I had two knives in my back. I still remember it."

Gringold coughed again. "Fellow, you can't just walk out on us. Give a little, for God's sake. You're inhuman. The dough I got is blood squeezed out of my own pores. Take it and let's start working on the picture."

Webster laid the telephone on the *concierge's* table. He lighted a cigarette, exhaled, and picked up the telephone again. "Send over the money," he said, "and when I come back we'll talk."

"Okay, fellow, that's great. You're a real sport. But couldn't you possibly have a little chit-chat with us at dinner tonight?"

"No."

"Well," Gringold said, reluctantly. "I'll send around a runner with the check. Francs okay?"

"If that's what you've got."

"Couldn't get dollars on such short notice. Had to lay out a pile of dough to get Suzette tested. Web, she's terrific. Never seen a camera before, but she's a natural. I see her in something like *Open City;* you know—slit skirt and a torn blouse. She's sexier than Monroe. Think about it like that. Raw, untrained, but lots of bust. A tit show."

"I'll think about it."

"Good boy. The check's on its way. Hurry back."

Webster replaced the telephone, tipped the *concierge* and walked out to the street.

Tomorrow he would be with Hil at a place on the Côte he had never seen. In more than two years he had not had a real vacation, and he told himself that he ought to make the most of this one. They would have a room together and there would be a beach and in the evenings he could write.

At the rue de Vaugirard he turned to walk toward the Luxembourg Gardens but the smell of coffee from a *brasserie* stopped him and he ordered a *fine café*.

Watching Sorbonne students with their books and notes he thought of the student atmosphere in which he lived. If he lived on the Right Bank, say in the Eighth Arrondissement, he would be out of that environment and in another completely different. There would be the wealthy coming and going to the Crillon; diplomats from the American and British Embassies; the *poules* on the Boulevard des Capucines; bookstalls along the rue de Rivoli and the shaded bridle-path of the Avenue Gabriel.

With a little more money he could afford to live there—a few blocks off the Champs-Élysées—even though that would bring him near Tay. Life would be more comfortable on the Right Bank. He could have a presentable apartment, even a cook. To live on the Left Bank you had to be very rich or very poor. If you were rich enough you could ignore the background of poverty, but if you were not yet poor the Left Bank tried to equalize you; drag you down with the others.

A month on the Côte should make him feel himself again, and he would be able to forget the fiasco with Tay. It took money to get to the Côte and more money to stay and play. You would be taken at your own face value, at least for a time. There would probably be some screen people he knew, and if he could work out a deal on the Côte there would be no need of seeing Kress and Gringold again.

He stirred his coffee, and thought, so much for daydreaming. It was useless because it never paid off. If he had dreamed over his books in college he would still be there; hoping, waiting for something to happen. His problem had been the thing with Lee going bad just when the studios were cutting down. He had tried to hold together his marriage when he should have been trying to see that he was not cut out of work. But the marriage had failed, anyway, and the work had fallen off until, in the end, there was nothing for him at all.

The house had been the first to go, and he had moved to an apartment on the hill above the Strip. Then had come the women contract players, bar girls, bored movie wives, and he had been a good companion ... he remembered a long weekend at Malibu with the wife of an executive producer. She had gone to Switzerland for face and breast uplift surgery, and the surgeon had given her the high, tight breasts of a much younger girl. The scars that were left were only small white lines, no wider than the mark of a pencil. But after Malibu the woman had told her friends, and the executive producer must have heard about it because Webster was never hired again at his studio.

There had been no good reason for the Malibu interlude, or if there had been at the time, he could not remember what it was. The woman and her husband had divorced much later, and both of them had married again; the woman to a senior at U.C.L.A.

There was nothing to be gained from raking over the old, cold ashes. He knew that he would not have looked back into the past if he had not come across Tay and her grandmother, and he should have realized that they should have been left to themselves.

When he paid the waiter he walked back along the Rue de Vaugirard to Raspail and got his laundry from the *blanchisserie.* Carrying the newspaper-wrapped parcel under his arm he went back up to his flat, opened up a suitcase and began to pack.

Walking through the acrid smoke of the station, Webster heard the rumble of trains arriving and departing. He stopped at a stand to buy a bottle of Monnet and followed his porter through the gate toward the platform where the *wagon-lit* waited. He walked slowly, looking upward at the naked roof girders where pigeons nested, and when he had reached his section, he waited while the porter carried his bags on board and came out again.

The porter said, "*Nombre quatre, m'sieu.*"

"*Merci.*" Webster tipped the porter.

Webster looked at his watch and saw that he had six minutes before departure time. He lighted a Bleu and leaned against a baggage cart watching people board the train. Only a few older people were getting into the *wagon-lit.* Most of the travelers were younger, and they came as mixed pairs or in coveys of teen-aged girls with lunch baskets and tickets in their hands. Visitors were embracing travelers, and Webster began to feel lonely. He took the Monnet from his pocket, uncorked it, and drank. The cognac tasted rich and full and burned his throat only a little. He drank again, and put the cork back into the bottle, thinking that the cognac would help him to sleep. Traveling alone was something he had never enjoyed, and so he preferred to travel at night. On longer trips he liked to play cards or read and drink, but tomorrow afternoon he would leave the *wagon-lit at* Nice, and the train journey would be over.

He thought of the check in his pocket and forgot the loneliness that had come over him. A messenger had brought it while Webster was packing, and it was for nearly seven hundred thousand francs; enough to pay for the holiday unless Hil played the wheel at Monaco. He threw his cigarette under the *wagon-lit* and walked toward the boarding steps. She could use her own money to gamble.

Webster walked along the passageway until he came to his compartment, opened the door and went inside. The porter had left his bags on the berth, and Webster lifted one to the luggage rack. He opened the other and took out his pajamas, dressing robe and shaving kit. Then he placed the bag on the luggage rack and poured cognac into a glass. He added tap water, stirred the drink with his finger and sat on the seat, looking out of the window.

On the platform below, porters pushed empty baggage carts back toward the Gare. A few people waved upward at the *wagon-lit* windows, and the train began to move.

Webster watched through the window until the train cleared the yards, and then he pulled down the curtain, shutting out the diminishing lights of Paris. The motion seemed to have finality and as he finished his drink, it seemed as though he had left nothing behind.

7.

HILDRETH MET HIM ON THE PLATFORM AT NICE. He saw her before the train had stopped, her black hair gleaming in the sun; dark glasses, sandals, and a bandeau above her print skirt. She waved at him as he stepped down to the platform, and kissed him quickly.

"I thought you'd never come, darling."

"I only got your wire yesterday morning."

"How's Paris?"

"About the same."

She held his hand tightly, and put her other arm around him until the porter came out of Webster's compartment with his bags. Then she led them to a parked Lancia roadster and the porter put the bags into the small trunk.

"Yours?" Webster asked.

"Yes. I bought it last week. I thought it might be fun to have."

"It looks like great fun," Webster said. He got behind the wheel, tipped the porter, and said, "How's life on the Riviera, Hil."

"Just wonderful. You won't know how wonderful it is until you've been here a while. I never want to go back to Paris again."

"You don't have to," he said, and started the engine.

Hildreth pointed out the way to the coast road, and when they had left Nice, she said, "I've rented the sweetest little place for us. On the side of the hill facing the ocean. We've got a cook and a gardner, and I know you'll love it." She moved against him and kissed the side of his face. "I've missed you, darling. It's been a long time. Never so long before."

"We'll make up for it," he said. "I even brought my own money."

"It wasn't necessary."

"It worked out that way; Paul and Henri paid me something on account."

"And did you sell your story?"

"I didn't write it."

"I'm sorry, Web. But I'm interested in everything you do." She kissed his throat. "We should have more in common than just bedtime."

He drove the Lancia carefully around the hairpin *corniches* that dropped off sheerly into ocean inlets below. Above them on the terraced hillside he could see the greenness of low Aleppo pines, cork trees and cypress stand out from the sand-colored background. The air was hot and very dry. Overnight he had come from the autumn humidity of Paris to the semi-tropical Riviera and the dry heat braced him. He took off his tie and opened his collar.

Hil said, "The sun's been absolutely marvelous. I can't wait to go swimming with you. Would you feel up to it so soon?"

"Whenever you say."

She leaned back and closed her eyes so that the sun was directly on her face. "We have our own little cove where no one will bother us. Even my breasts are tanned. I feel completely marvelous."

"I feel lousy."

"You won't say that tomorrow, darling. We'll have a wonderful afternoon in the water, and a long, long night."

Then they came around a turn, and Hildreth leaned forward and pointed above them toward the hill. "There's Eze," she said. "It looks just like a fortress, doesn't it? The way it clings almost frightens me."

Below the town the cliffs dropped steeply away into the ocean where waves broke against the rocky base.

She said, "We're on the other side."

They drove through the town, and she showed him where to turn down to a narrow road that ended above the ocean at a small house of coral-colored stucco. There was a small, crescent-shaped beach below the house's hillside garden, and to the east a deep, narrow *calanque* where the ocean entered.

To the south the Mediterranean glittered greenly in the afternoon sun. The reflection was so strong that his eyes hurt. From the foot of the garden a barebacked man came toward them. Sweat glistened on his arms and chest and he wiped his forehead with a colored handkerchief. Webster lifted his bags from the trunk and Hildreth said, "This is Jean, the gardner. He's been awfully useful."

"Bon jour," Webster said.

"Bon jour, m'sieu." He picked up the bags and walked toward the house.

Hildreth said, "Let's get undressed right away. It's too lovely an afternoon to waste."

Web followed her into the house, and the bedroom was at the back of the house, facing into the hillside. When they were alone, Web took off his jacket and his shirt and lighted a cigarette.

Hildreth pointed to a bottle and some glasses on the table. "Drink?" she asked.

"Not now." He bent over to take off his shoes, and when he raised up again, he saw that Hildreth had dropped her bandeau. Her breasts swung heavily as she walked toward him. Then she undid her sandal thongs and unbuttoned her skirt. Her hands turned his face toward hers, and she said, "Now, darling. Just to steady ourselves." She lay back on the bed and wriggled free of the skirt. Her body was completely tanned. Its hair glinted like gold-colored silk.

Webster laid his cigarette in an ash tray and kissed her lips. Then her arms were around him and the hot moistness of her body and her nails gouging into his flanks as he began to take her, and in the darkened room there was only the sound of her breath as it caught in her throat.

Then, when they were spent, they lay together, sharing the last of Webster's cigarette until strength and reality returned, and he knew that for both it had been full and complete and unendingly satisfying, erasing the memory of the abrupt shallowness he had felt the last time with her in Paris.

Hildreth got up and walked to a bureau drawer. She took out a two-piece Bikini suit and slipped on the bandeau. She looked back at Webster, and said, "God, that was wonderful, Web. I couldn't have lasted another day without you."

Or someone, he thought, as he sat up and opened one of his bags. He took out his trunks, and watched Hildreth lace a loin cloth around her thighs. He felt purged and unaggressive and a little sleepy.

They walked down to the beach together, and lying on the sand beside her, Webster fell asleep.

As he slept Hildreth poured oil onto his shoulders and his back and smoothed it into a film with her hands. She kneaded the muscles of his shoulders and his arms, and then she lay back and bared her breasts to the sun. She oiled her body and her face, and took off her dark sun glasses. She felt for his hand, and holding it she felt herself drift into sleep.

Webster woke first and saw that the sun was lower than when they had reached the beach. His throat was dry with thirst, and he walked back into the kitchen and took two bottles of cold beer from the icebox. He opened them and went back down to the beach. Hildreth was sitting up then, oiling her arms again, and when she saw him, she said, "I began to think I'd only dreamed you were here." She smiled. "How foolish of me—I remember perfectly well."

He gave her a bottle of beer and sat down beside her, seeing where the light wind had drifted sand onto her oiled body.

Because the sun was lower the ocean had silvered and he knew that it would not be green and blue again until the morning.

She took the bottle from her lips, and said, “You’ve never been on the Mediterranean before, have you, Web?”

“As a matter of fact, I have; but on the other side.”

“Africa?”

He nodded and drank from the bottle. “North Africa. Morocco, Algeria, Tunisia and Egypt.”

“I forgot you fought there.”

“With a million other men. It was the big show for a while, and then when it was over, everyone forgot it.”

“Except the ones who died.”

“Yes,” he said. “Except those.” He put his knees together and closed his eyes. “There was a little beach not far from Bizerte that smelled like this part of the Mediterranean. In the evening we’d drive our tanks down into the water to wash them and cool them, and dive from their turrets. The water was warm and clear and the way it felt to be rid of dust and dirt and sandflies was something I’ll never forget.”

“Better than a woman?” she asked, half-smiling.

“Yes,” he said. “Even better than a woman.” He opened his eyes and drank again, and the told beer revived him and slaked his thirst and he watched drops of perspiration force their way through the oil on his body, flow together and drop quickly onto the sand. The sun and the beer made him feel lightheaded. When he had finished the beer, he stood up and pulled Hildreth to her feet. She started to pick up her bandeau, but he said, “You won’t need it. We’ll swim over to the cove.”

Hildreth laughed and began running ahead of him into the water. He followed, watching it rise from her ankles to her legs and then her thighs, splashing higher, until she fell forward and began swimming away from him toward the deep *calanque* that would shelter them from sight of the house. He began to run into the water, lifting his knees high as the water deepened, until the water seemed to suck him into it, and then he dove forward, pulling himself underwater, gliding close to the clear bottom until he had to surface for air.

As he swam he could see Hildreth ahead of him, her arms cutting cleanly into the water, her feet fluttering regularly in crawl rhythm. They rounded the point of the beach and let the current carry them into the apex of the cove. Opening his eyes underwater he could see that the bottom was not sandy but pebbled, and the narrow shore was a litter of boulders that had fallen from above or been cut from the wall of the cove by the action of the waves.

A large flat rock slanted down into the water and Hildreth pulled herself up onto it. As she stood watching Webster she began to wring out her hair. Then she drew it back behind her shoulders and sat down on the rock until he had climbed up beside her. His breathing drew deeply, and he could feel the beating of his heart as he lay back against the warm stone.

He said, "Where did you learn to swim?"

"In Lake Michigan. It's much colder, you know. You swim fast to keep warm." She looked down at her breasts and touched them. "That's why I've got good breasts." She squinted up at the sun, and began unlacing her loincloth. She raised herself to be free of it, and then she lay back beside Webster. "How do you feel now?" she asked.

"Fine." He felt her fingers begin to pull at his trunks, and she said, "I want you to be as tanned as I am."

"Maybe the sun will sterilize me."

"So much the better." She laid his trunks on the rock beside her loincloth. Then she moved against him. "Oh, Web, I'm so happy now you're with me. Let's never go back to Paris."

"You've got a husband."

She shook her head. "I've forgotten him. I owe nothing to anyone."

He felt her lips touch his shoulder, and her fingers were winding themselves into his wet hair. "Neither do I," he said.

She began to move against him slowly and rhythmically, and then she fitted herself to him so that it was easy and slow and not tiring at all, and around them was only the warmth of the air and the sound of water against the rock below.

The day ended for them on the terrace with champagne in an iced bucket and a light evening wind from the ocean that stirred the corners of the table linen and brought with it a memory of water and sun and sand. Beyond the promontory that was Eze, the sun, burned out and dying, sank toward the edge of the sea, and in the distance they could see the sails of fishing boats that were coming back, now, toward Nice.

As he drank, he looked at the woman's profile, well-formed and beautiful, and he thought that to have known he would be here with her now would have helped him during the war when the African coast of the same ocean meant nothing but death and fear and pain.

Or with any woman, he thought; not necessarily this one with her excellent swimmer's breasts and her athlete's body that only American women ever really have. The months would have gone by more quickly and the war would not have been what it was to me if I had known that I would survive and in ten years be sitting on a terrace watching a Mediterranean sunset with a woman who makes love as capably as this one.

But now, preferably, Hildreth, who smoked in silence and watched the ocean grow calm, the breeze lifting the hair beside her ear and dropping it slowly as it passed.

As he watched the sea, a memory formed in his mind of a beach near Tunis, white-hot in the desert sun. He saw again the scalloped shore and the pyramidal tents of the mess-hall and barracks, and offshore the rusted, beached transport that had been dive-bombed by the Germans. The stores had been taken off the ship and the ship's beer and vegetables had gone quickly, but two hundred cases of rubber prophylactics had been stacked ashore in the sun where they melted in the heat and stank like burning tires.

The ship had been beached at an angle, and sometimes in the evenings they swam out to it and climbed a frayed Jacob's ladder to dive naked over the canting, rust-flaked bow into the deep, clear water; then, letting the dry air towel their bodies as they lay on the salt-bleached planking, gulls wheeling above and fiddler crabs darting around the scuppers. He remembered the heat of Tunis, sleeping naked on his cot, wearing khaki shorts and tank boots and a gabardine ball cap; the sun-warm Lyster bags and the brackish taste of Halazone purifier; dry pancakes without syrup or butter, old powdered eggs that smelled worse than the rotting condoms; C-rations and black Arabian coffee and a soul-deep craving for an iced Tom Collins and a cool seat beside an electric fan. One night the Germans had come over and dropped a stick of bombs near the headquarters encampment and the only thing they had killed was the mascot, a black-and-white terrier with long awkward legs that used to swim with them to the beached ship, and when the bomb explosions were over there was the scream of the dog dying with its legs torn off and a slab of shrapnel like a meat cleaver spilling its belly onto the sand.

He remembered the stink of North Africa, the old piss-smell of mud villages, the stink of offal in the sun, the clogging scent of cactus flowers at night, and the over-ripe odor of old straddle-trenches buried too shallowly. There was the memory of bombers taking off at night, their orange exhausts hissing and twisting like burning dragons, or the loneliness of a bombers' dawn when they left the airstrip half-buried in mist, and the sick fascination of a flaming bomber coming back, trying to make the strip, but crashing instead offshore with only a jet of steam to show where it had sunk. The welter of torn and bleeding aircrew men, their blistered flesh glistening like peanut brittle; of bandages that could not sop the gouts of blood; the vomit and the reek of death as chunks of bodies were carried away in basket stretchers...

All of it had been the war as he had known it, and the ending had come as a surprise, much later, outside Carvaggio in Lombardy with ragged *partisani* from the hills and bottles of marsala and steaming piles of spaghetti and the look of defeat on the faces of the conquered.

She turned from the sea to look at him, and said, "It's beautiful, isn't it? Truly beautiful, Web."

"Very beautiful. And silent."

"It's always silent."

"Now," he said, "but not always."

"I like the silence, too. I react miserably to noise, I'm afraid. It makes me terribly tense. I'll never be able to face the sound of Paris again."

"It's part of the necessary background," Webster said. "It isn't like New York."

"No. But I've become too fond of the silence here."

He said, "There's always the sound of the ocean. And the gulls and the wind."

"It's a background I like. It's soothing and it doesn't force itself on you."

"No."

She held her glass toward him, and he filled it. Then she said, "Do you know, Web, for someone I make love with so freely I know very little about you. I don't even know where you were born."

"I suppose not," he said. "I was born near Binghamton."

"Where's that?"

"New York."

"Oh. What was it like?"

"It was a small town," he said, "probably smaller than any you've ever seen."

"I've seen some very small ones."

"Yes—residential suburbs. But in my small town the high school was the biggest thing next to the Odd Fellows and the Grange."

"Really?"

"And there was a river and a swimming hole near the cemetery where I marched every Decoration Day parade."

"I can't imagine you marching in parades. Why did you?"

"The town thought a lot of its dead. The first World War was the biggest thing that ever happened to the town where I was born. Decoration Day was a day of marches and flags and speeches and all-day lunches at the Odd Fellows Hall served by the Legion Auxiliary."

"I always thought you came from New York City."

"When I learned to play the bugle I used to play Taps every Decoration Day at the cemetery; not where people could see me, but over the side of the hill beside the river."

"Not Robert Webster."

"Definitely Robert Webster. People used to look forward to the ceremony and I did too, and even my first year in college I missed it a little. You see, I thought that particular war was something everyone should have been in, and I hadn't been born until it was over. Playing Taps was the only contribution I could make, and after the Guard of Honor fired the salute, they'd give me their empty shells. I didn't know they were only blanks." He paused. "I wonder who plays Taps now on Decoration Day and whether anyone bothers to pick up the shells any more."

In his mind was the memory of his lips against the silver-plated mouthpiece that he had warmed carefully in his hand so that the first note would be true, and the phrasing he had rehearsed carefully so that the notes wolud be full and pure and holding high through the pines, then drifting slowly and softly away until there was only a memory of what he had played in tribute to men he had never known.

"Have you ever gone back?" she asked.

"No."

"Why not?"

"I outgrew it. I went to Columbia and learned Chaucer and philosophy and I learned to be ashamed of ever having known a town as small as that one."

"You aren't ashamed of it now."

"No," he said. "Not now. Not here, talking about it with you." He lighted a cigarette. "I learned to swim in the town swimming hole and each spring I caught sunfish at the foot of the falls. In the winter I ran a trapline for muskrat along the river; it meant getting up before sunrise and going to each trap every morning."

"What on earth did you do with the muskrats?"

"I sold them. To Sears and Roebuck for twenty-five cents a skin."

"You actually skinned them?" Hildreth asked.

"Of course."

"And how long were you a trapper, Web?"

"Until someone stole my traps. It wiped me out."

"Poor Web. What a tragedy it must have been," she said, half-seriously.

"One of my first." He exhaled smoke and watched it shroud the copper sun.

She said, quietly. "I've never known you."

"Most people never really know each other. My wife thought I was someone else entirely. She had her own picture of me, and she liked it that way. It would have been too complicated to try to change it."

"And then she wouldn't have been happy."

"No. She was seldom happy, as it was." He filled his glass, and drank it, watching gulls hover and dive at the entrance of the cove where the tide was running. "We pretend to be what we're not. I'm supposed to be a successful Hollywood screen writer picking up some French francs and enjoying a Continental vacation. Kress and Gringold pretend to be a couple of successful motion picture producers. A successful banker goes to a night club, puts on a paper hat and pretends to be a fool."

"And I pretend to be a wife."

He looked at her, and said, "Yes, I suppose you do."

"But I haven't really been; not for a long time."

"You ought to get rid of him if you don't like him."

"I didn't say that. I'm very fond of Frederic. He's a good companion now and then, and we don't fight ever. We don't care enough about each other to quarrel." She put her hand over his, and said, "I think I would be foolish to leave Frederic unless you loved me. We're happy, you and I, the way we are. But I think sometimes that you don't really approve of me."

Webster said, "No one approves of not staying by a bargain."

"A bargain like marriage?"

"Yes."

"Frederic didn't stand by his part of it, either; a long time before I began not to."

He sipped his champagne and looked at the rings on her fingers. "Well," he said, "I suppose that makes it all right."

Then, before the light left the ocean the cook came out to the terrace, wiping her hands on her apron, and said that dinner was ready if madame and m'sieu would please come inside and not stay outside in the wind and catch cold.

The dinner began with a soup of sea-nettles and shellfish, then coq au vin with small white potatoes and crisply-cooked vegetables, and ended with Camembert and coffee. It was as good as anything but the food of the best Paris restaurants, and afterward they took the Lancia and drove down along the ocean drive toward Monaco, where lights sparkled through the fronds of tall palms along the drive. The air was cool and sweet and it had the clean smell of the sea and the heavier, mixed perfumes of mimosa, jasmine, orange and violets.

Webster asked, "Does it ever snow here?"

Hildreth laughed. "It did once. About twenty-five years ago. Why?"

"A friend of mine wants it to snow while I'm here. He thinks I treated him badly."

"Did you?"

"Probably."

They drove through Monaco and almost to Menton on the Italian border, before turning around, and taking the same road back toward Eze. The moon was high above them, then, and it lighted a broad path on the ocean. Webster could have seen the way even without the Lancia's headlights.

As he stopped the car beside the house, he asked, "Tired, Hil?"

"A little. But I'd still like a drink."

He made highballs in the living room, and they sat smoking quietly, tired from the afternoon, feeling pleasantly relaxed from the drive, and then, in a little while, they turned out the lights and went to bed.

8.

RINO UNLOCKED THE DOOR OF HIS HOUSE on the Villa Saïd and stood aside to let Tay come in. He closed the door, helped her out of her jacket and laid it across the back of a chair. Then he followed her into the living room, turned on a table lamp and opened the glass door to the terrace.

A butler came in from the hallway to inquire if anything was wanted, and Rino asked, "Café, darling?"

Tay said, "Just a demi-tasse," and took a cigarette from a silver bowl. As Rino lighted it she could see above the lighter flame the bank of Rino's racing pictures on the wall. There were photographs of long, powerful-looking racing cars with Rino behind the wheel or standing near the radiator with a trophy. Checkered racing flags were crossed above the fireplace, and over them hung a painted escutcheon. Tay walked slowly to the fireplace and touched one of the flags. Her fingers felt its coarse muslin fabric with dirt and grease imbedded among the fibers. Then she turned away and leaned back against the mantel.

She said, "It's very late, isn't it?"

"It's late, but I thought you would stay here tonight."

She moved her head negatively. "I'm too tired tonight, Rino. And I've developed a dreadful headache."

"After coffee you may feel better."

"Perhaps."

The butler brought in the coffee tray with a bottle of Bisquit. He lowered the tray to the coffee table, filled two demi-tasses, and asked, "Will there be anything else tonight?"

"No. Not tonight."

"Good night, sir; madame."

"Good night," Rino said. He lifted the bottle of Bisquit from the tray and asked, "Cognac?"

"Yes, but only a little."

He added the cognac to their coffee and carried a demi-tasse to Tay. "Sorry you're off form tonight."

"It may be only a mood."

He kissed her lips, and said, "I sensed that even at dinner you were not quite yourself."

"I'm sorry if I've spoiled your evening."

He said, "Each of us has different moods, and it is often better not to inquire their cause. Then they may go away."

He turned on the big record player, and for a while they listened to its music. Then he kissed her lips again, and said, "Before the *Rallye* I want you to see me drive."

"I'll see you in the *Rallye*."

"Yes. And you'll love Nice. You should have seen it long ago. The Promenade des Anglais is really memorable. Now we'll see it together." His lips brushed the back of her hand. "I wanted you to stay with me tonight, Tay."

"Please, Rino," she said. "It's late and I'm feeling wretched." She stood up, and said, "You won't have to drive me home. There'll be a taxi at Porte Maillot."

"I wouldn't think of it." He brought her jacket and helped her into it. Then he opened the front door and followed her through the garden to the Boulevard de l'Amiral Bruix where he had left his Fiat sportster.

Driving up the Avenue de la Grande Armée he put his arm around her shoulders and drew her to him. He kissed her hair.

Near the Étoile they looked up at the Arc de Triomphe, massive and gray against the dark sky. Along the Champs-Élysées the tables and chairs of sidewalk cafés were stacked under the shadows of canopies, and because the gendarmes had left, a few *poules* lingered near cabaret entrances.

At Rond Point he turned onto the Avenue Matignon and the Fiat pulled easily into the Place des Saussaies. Before Tay got out of the Fiat they kissed good-night and he said that he would call her in the morning.

She stood in front of her door watching him drive away down the rue des Saussaies, and when the tail light of the Fiat was lost she unlocked the door and went up to her apartment.

Lying in bed she watched the shadows on the ceiling for a long time, and then she began, unreasonably, to cry.

In the morning they were at the beach early while the tide still ebbed and the wind was cool against their bodies. They swam into the cove and Webster had a face mask and a barbed steel rod, but the only fish he saw were small ones, not worth the chase, and he knew that the larger fish would not come into the cove until the tide turned in the afternoon.

They lay on the big rock letting the sun dry their bodies, the light wind like gentle fingers against their skin, and Hildreth said, "Would you mind going to the Casino tonight?"

"No."

"I want you to play, too. I'll stake you."

"It wouldn't be the same. I'll play bird-cage."

"That's such a common game, Web. You can't win very much. Where's your gambling blood?"

"At a thousand francs a throw I can't lose much, either."

Hildreth made a face. "The Casino isn't any fun unless you play baccarat or the wheel."

"Hil," he said, "I'll watch you play as long as you care to. But I can't afford the same games. Is it something worth quarreling over?"

"No. Not at all. And you won't mind?"

"No."

"There'll be stimulating people there, too. Quite a few British."

"Jolly," he said, dryly. "Awfully jolly."

"Don't be hostile, darling. British men are really very amusing; they have such filthy minds and they go to such extremes to hide it. When they think their wives aren't looking they're always taking you aside and whispering something dreadfully obscene."

"That doesn't make them different."

She looked at him reflectively. "No. Except you, you sensual bastard. You didn't even proposition me. You just took me."

Webster said, "We've been all over that night before."

"Indeed we have. And we'll go through it many times more. I like to remember it. It had elements of novelty."

He turned on his side and closed his eyes. As the sun warmed him he felt the bitterness and failure of Paris drain out of him. When you were relaxed and at ease with your environment there was no room for memories of failure. He should have come here a long time ago, when things first began going wrong, and let the sun and the sea restore him. As he thought back, nothing seemed as important now as it had in Paris; not the bad picture nor the money nor Tay Crandall. They were all still there, but when he went back, finally, he would be able to see everything clearly and in proportion.

Hil asked, "Have I ever seen any of your pictures, darling?"

"Probably." He named three of the better ones.

"Yes, I've seen those. And I liked them, too. They were very good. You'd like to do a good picture in France, wouldn't you?"

"I'd like to do one anywhere. I had a chance with Kress and Gringold, but they aborted it."

"You'd rather not talk about it, I guess."

"It doesn't help. It just makes me feel lousy."

"I'm sorry."

He turned over onto his belly, and felt her hand find his.

Until the wind died away and the sun grew too hot, they lay drowsily, and then they slipped down into the cooling water to swim back to the beach.

At the Casino that night Hildreth lost nearly a hundred thousand francs and Webster won a total of six thousand at bird-cage and vingt-et-un. They had a late supper with two British couples who were spending pounds sterling smuggled out of England in corsets and hollowed-out books, and a Swiss chemist and his wife. The conversation seemed excessively trivial, and while he was dancing with Hildreth, Webster said, "I've had about all the Continental atmosphere I can handle. Would you mind if we left?"

"Not everyone has your brilliant mind, darling. You could try to be tolerant of other people. Even of me."

He said, "Your friends are dull, Hil. I've been reasonable with them. I haven't embarrassed you."

"Because you've kept our little secret that we aren't really married, and I'm just someone you brought here for the screwing?"

"That's not what I meant."

"The hell it isn't. I know what you really think of me." Her body stiffened under his hand.

He said, "You've had enough for tonight. If you can't lose money any better than that you ought not to gamble at all."

"Everything went against me. It wasn't fair."

"It's never fair. That's why the Casino is so big and beautiful. You've got a twenty per cent chance against you when you walk into the room."

"You know everything, don't you?"

He said, "Shall we stay and watch Hildreth get slapped or will we leave now, before I get to liking the idea?"

She moved her head back and stared at him. "You ought to slap me anyway," she said. "I'm in a poisonous mood."

"You certainly are."

"We'll go, Web." She leaned her head against his shoulder. "Sorry I'm such a poor loser."

"You're too accustomed to winning," he said, and led her away from the dance floor. The Swiss chemist was alone at the table, and he stood up when Hildreth reached the table.

She said, "We're going now."

"But so early?"

"We've spent all our money," Webster said.

Hildreth took her bag from the table and gave him her hand.

The Swiss bent over it briefly, and asked, "You will return tomorrow evening?"

"Definitely not," Hildreth said. "We're going ballooning by moonlight."

"Ballooning, my dear?"

"Of course. We've promised ourselves a definitive look at the Alpes Maritimes without the vexing noise of airplane propellors. A balloon is simply ideal. Would you join us?"

He shook his head. "I regret that we leave in the morning by car to tour the Rhone valley. You have seen it before?"

"I've seen it," Hildreth said. "It's lovely and serene and as dull as death." She smiled at him, and said, "Thank you for the lovely conversation."

"A pleasure, madame." The Swiss bowed stiffly and as they left the table, the music ended, and Webster saw the two British couples begin to walk from the dance floor toward the Swiss chemist.

In the Lancia, Webster said, "Why the change of heart?"

She shrugged. "You were right. They were savage bores, all of them." She turned toward him and kissed the side of his cheek. "You've spoiled me, darling. I'm becoming dependent upon you even though I try not to. Unfortunately, most of the people I'll see the rest of my life will be just as tiresome as the ones we just left."

"You deserve better than that."

"Do I?" She looked away from him. "I'm not sure I deserve anything at all. If I hadn't had money and an urge to live in

Europe I might have become a moderately successful housewife in Kankakee who brought her husband's pipe and slippers every night, trembled at his least word, and did the family wash on Mondays."

"And belonged to the P.T.A."

"Perhaps—if the Junior League would let me."

Webster said, "Is it so thoroughly repulsive, Hil?"

"It's mediocrity. I'm not used to mediocrity; I've grown used to cleverness. Even a little viciousness."

"A little."

He felt her hand turn his head until he was looking at her. She said, quietly, "I'd hate to find myself in love with you one morning. God, how I'd hate that."

"Is there any danger?"

"There's more than there ought to be, but so far I haven't faced it." Her hand touched his arm and she said, "Ah, Web, you'd never love me the way I'd love you. Not ever. Not even if we lived together this way for a thousand years."

"It would be a fine thousand years."

"Yes. Wouldn't it, though."

They drove the rest of the way back to Eze, and when he had braked the Lancia, Hildreth said, "I want to go swimming. My little hangover will go away if I do." She stepped out of the car, and said, "Unbutton me, darling. Ladies first."

He helped her out of the dress and watched her drop it across the back of the seat. Then he took off his dinner clothes and they walked down to the beach together.

Before they went into the water, they watched its restless motion under the moon and the fire-like phosphorescence of swells that did not break and become waves. Hand in hand they walked into water that was warmer than the air and when it had reached Webster's shoulders Hildreth put her hands around his neck and let herself drift with the motion of the sea until her legs came around his body and held them together until she was ready to drift free again.

As she floated backward he saw her breasts above the surface like distant, separate islands, that promised rest and nourishment and pleasure to their discoverer. Only a moment before they had been part of the water together and part of each other without any sense of weight or purposeful motion, and her eyes were closed under the moonlight as though he had killed her. With a sense of unreality he began to swim toward her to take her hand and bring them back to shore.

Two weeks of sun and water tanned his body and gave tone to his muscles. A note from Roland said that he had signed a *Syndicat* contract with Cygne Productions, and he urged Webster to make a story synopsis for Kress and Gringold in Paris. Webster showed the letter to Hildreth who read it and asked, "Shouldn't you start writing again?"

"Yes. I should."

"But not all the time, darling."

"No."

They walked out of the post office, and on the street Webster watched a man pasting up a poster that announced the October racing-car *Rallye.*

Hildreth noticed it, and said, "There's something we ought to see."

"We won't be here."

"We could stay, Web. I have no reason to go back to Paris. Frederic's only written three letters since I've been gone. He writes me on Sunday nights and it's a great effort."

"You've seen races before."

"Not ones that go right through towns and over turns like these *corniches.* My God, it must be thrilling to see."

"See it, then," Webster said, "but I'll be back in Paris."

"I want you to stay on with me. You like it here, and the house is certainly comfortable enough."

"It's fine," he said. "Everything's fine."

"You could start writing tonight."

"All right."

"If you leave, it won't be the same. Without you, it won't be anything at all. What am I supposed to do then?"

"Whatever you want," he said. He stopped at a flower stall and bought some violets for her.

She took them, and said, "Is this supposed to make up for you going away?"

"No. I thought you might like them."

"I do," she said. "My lover has bought me some violets. He notices me. He thinks flowers go well with my eyes."

"They do."

She clipped them against the side of her hair, and said, "Oh, Web, I know I'm unreasonable but I can't help it. I know you'll have to go but I don't have to be happy about it."

"No," he said. "I'm not happy about it either." He opened the door of the Lancia for her, and held it while she got in behind the wheel. She looked up at him, and said, "Let's make the most of being together, darling. I can't help feeling we'll never have it again."

"Why shouldn't we?" He sat down on the seat beside her.

"Just a feeling. Before we met I'd had the feeling I was going to meet someone like you. Now I feel it isn't going to last much longer."

He lighted a cigarette, and said, "Want to go back to the beach?"

"Do you?"

"We could go over to Nice and drink on the Promenade des Anglais. Or watch the jugglers in the Esplanade de Gaulle."

"It's too hot to watch jugglers. Let's just go home and get drunk. Or you can write and I'll get drunk."

He nodded, and they drove down through Eze, Webster seeing more *Rallye* posters, remembering that Rino Menotti would be driving in the race and that Tay Crandall would be in Nice with him for the *Rallye*. He had not let himself think of Tay, but now a single colored poster brought her back to his mind.

While Hildreth drove, he thought, the thing with Hil is not complicated the way it would have been with Tay. Hil's had time to make up her mind about the kind of life she wants, but Tay is only beginning to find out. Hil knows how little there is to faith and trust, and even love. What Hil does is a way of life she's chosen and she knows everything that it means. But Tay doesn't really know what kind of life she wants for herself. So she'll sleep around and in time she'll end up brittle and modern like Hil.

Only I hope that she doesn't, he said to himself. I don't want her to be like Hil.

When they got to the house the gardener was raking the beach and the cook had gone to market in Eze. Webster made Scotch highballs with Vittel and chipped ice and they sat under the terrace canopy in the still warmth of the afternoon. He lay back against the cushioned lounge chair, and it seemed to him that he had done this many times before with women he could not now remember, with the drinking and the not-serious talk and the feeling of tremendous well-being that was the same in Palm Springs and Santa Barbara as it was now, in Eze.

As he looked back on those times, they were not well begun nor well ended, and they represented days and months that had been a waste of life except for the good liquor that had been drunk and the beautiful bodies that had brought pleasure to his.

Hildreth made herself another drink and sat down on a hassock in the shade. She said, "The sound of ice in a glass is one of the prettiest in the world, isn't it, Web?"

"Particularly when someone else is buying the drinks."

She laughed and said, "Tell me another pretty sound, darling. You should be able to think of a lot of them."

Webster looked at his drink, and held it out in the sunlight so that the ice became a prism splitting the light into colors. "Rain on the roof," he said. "On a spring night when there's no snow on the ground and you know in the morning everything will be green for the first time since winter."

"That's visual," she said. "Too visual. I mean something I don't have to think about."

"All right; a piano being played at three in the morning. You can't see it and you don't know where it is. You're walking along the street and the sound comes from somewhere high in a darkened apartment building. You've never heard the melody before and you never hear it again."

She shook her head. "Too musical. Something else."

"A waterfall deep in the forest."

"Good," she said. "More like that."

"The crunch of snow under your skis. There's a crust but new snow has fallen in the night and you're the first one on the trail."

"That's good, too. What else?"

"A plane engine coughing back to life in the air after it started to go bad."

"No. Too mechanical."

He said, "You're very demanding today."

"You're a creative guy. I expect you to do better than that."

"Summer wind in the leaves."

"At night, of course."

"Yes. At night."

"But it's awfully trite. Try again."

He thought for a while, and then he said, "The ring of a telephone when you've been waiting a long time for it."

She nodded. "Yes."

"The snap of frost in the timbers of a house."

"Only sometimes," she said. "It depends on the house."

"The way your line sings when a big fish runs with the hook."

"I suppose so."

"The whir of quail breaking cover before you see them."

"Also musical," she said, and finished her drink. "You must be able to think of others."

"The hell with you. The sound of a woman's throat when she reaches orgasm. The scratch of a pen when someone writes you a check. The crack of a shotgun on a perfect double." He looked at her. "Satisfied?"

She raised her eyebrows, and said, "Don't be violent, darling. You've had a lovely life. You should be very happy about it."

"The hell with my happy life."

"You're happier than practically anyone I know. I'll bet you've never even done anything you're really ashamed of. Nothing mean or really dirty."

"Like taking on a fairy?" he said. "No, I was never attracted."

"Tell me," she said. "Tell me what you've done that you could possibly be ashamed of."

Webster drank from his glass and put it down on the flagstone. He thought for a while, and then he said, "I was in New Orleans, before North Africa. We were getting ready to ship out, and while we were waiting we did a lot of drinking."

"You weren't married then?"

"No. But a captain I knew was, and his wife had come from Atlanta to stay with him until he left, and after his ship left I ran across her one night in the De Soto bar. She was alone and drunk and feeling like hell because he'd gone." He closed his eyes and remembered the warm moistness of New Orleans that night and the smell of smoke in the De Soto bar with everyone drinking Ramos Fizzes because it had been the thing to drink. He said, "So we did the jazz and gin joints until I got the idea she wanted to go to bed with me."

"Husband substitute," Hildreth said. "Happened all the time." She looked at him. "It still does."

He looked away from her. "Maybe she thought he was going to be killed, and she wanted to be the first to kill what they had together. To end it quickly."

"It could be that, too."

After a while, Webster said, "We went to her room for a few more drinks, and when I reached for her, she said no." He felt the muscles of his jaw stiffen. "She fought me but I forced her, and finally she relaxed and lay under me, staring up, not moving at all, or even crying. It was like doing it to a corpse. And when it was over I got off the bed and threw back her pants I'd torn off, but all she did was look at me and tell me she wanted to kill me for what I'd made her do."

"It wasn't all your fault."

"Not all. I could have stopped anytime; I wasn't in season. I knew I was screwing the wife of a friend against her will, and when I was leaving I heard her begin to pray he would be killed and not have to come back to her."

"The little fool; she actually thought you'd made a whore of her. But how does the story end? Was the captain killed?"

Webster shook his head. "I saw him in Leghorn before we left Italy."

Hildreth said, "By then she'd slept with twenty other guys and loved it."

"But I was the first," Webster said. "I forced her, so that afterward nothing woud have been quite as bad. After me she wouldn't have felt there was anything to lose."

"I'll bet she never told him."

"It was a long war," Webster said. "There was a lot of time for things to happen to a lot of people." He sat forward to make another drink, but Hildreth got up from the hassock and came toward him. She knelt between his legs and pulled down her shoulder straps. She touched her breasts, pressing them in, moulding them outward, letting their weight flatten them against her palms, and she said, "You don't have to force me, darling. Now or ever." She leaned forward, and let herself fall beside him so that he could turn and meet her lips. Her tongue searched his mouth possessively and she closed her eyes. Then, as they adjusted to each other, he remembered again the body and the eyes of the captain's wife, and the memory was like a sheath that deadened sensation and made him slow to respond.

9.

He began to make notes the next day, working on the beach while Hildreth lay in the sun beside him. They drank iced beer, and after lunch they swam for a while. When they were walking back to the sand again, Hildreth said, "You've been awfully quiet today, darling."

"I'm just trying to work."

"I know." She began squeezing her hair dry. Water ran down her tanned body onto the sand. She said, "It doesn't have to be all the time, does it?"

"I suppose not." He brushed water from his arms and pushed his hands through his hair.

"You hardly said a word to me all morning."

"I thought you were sleeping."

She shook her head and began to dry her face with a towel. "I wasn't. I was only pretending so you could work."

He sat down on the sand and watched her dry herself. The muscles of her arms and back played back and forth like ripples on smooth water. When she breathed, her breasts lifted high and a vault formed beneath them. He said, "You should have said something to me."

She dropped to her knees in front of him. "And disturb you?" Her hands held his shoulders and she said, "There must be a way that you can work and I can be with you without feeling I'm all alone."

"Tell me what you'd like."

She dropped her arms and looked at him. "I guess I won't ever be satisfied with just part of you, Web. When you're thinking, you're so distant from me that I'm frightened. This morning the thought of losing you made me turn cold."

"That isn't something to worry about."

She tilted her head and looked up at him. "I think about it all the time. I can't help it, darling. The way we are, there's no permanence; none at all. It isn't as if we were married."

"No."

"That's really a funny thing for me to say, because I'm married and there's nothing permanent about that."

"Isn't there?"

She shook her head, and sat back on her heels. "You know what my marriage has been. But now it's becoming inconvenient for me."

"In what way?"

She looked at him and then she touched her fingers to the sand. "You," she said. "That's all. You, Web. You must know how I feel about you."

"Tell me," he said. "Tell me how you feel."

Her hands brushed her breasts, and she said, "I love you. You must know that. I'm crazy about you, and I can't bear to think of losing you." She crawled forward to him and kissed the side of his cheek. "God, but I'm miserable. I love you and I want you and I don't know how you feel at all." She raised her head, and said, "Won't you tell me? I've got to know."

Webster looked at her long, tanned thighs. He said, "Do you want to marry me, Hil?"

"Yes," she said. "God, yes, darling. I'd do everything in the world to make you happy." She began to cry. Her shoulders and her body seemed to shudder. She pressed the back of his hand against her cheek. "Even if you don't really love me I could be so very happy with you."

He drew her to him and kissed her. "It could work out," he said. "There isn't any reason it couldn't."

"No. And even now we're happier than most married people ever are."

He nodded.

She lay against him for a while, and then she dried her eyes, and said, "I don't think Frederic will really care. I'll go back to Paris when you leave and talk with him. Then we can make our plans." She kissed his face and framed it with the palms of her hands. "I want you so much, Web. I'll be everything you could ever want in a woman."

Not everything, he thought, as he stood up and drew her to her feet, but you're still the best available. They walked up the path to the house.

In the bedroom with her then, it was not quite like any other time, but quick and searing and when it was over, there were tears on her cheeks.

They drove a few times to Eze for mail, and to Nice to watch the Promenade in the evenings and they danced at the Casino. Webster managed to work from the notes he had made that day on the beach, and as the story progressed he began to feel that if Kress and Gringold did not buy it, another producer or studio would. He had laid the background in Marseilles with a girl of the waterfront and two brothers who were in love with her. The setting of wharves and boats could be filmed on location without much cost and the interiors could be duplicated in the studio outside Paris. Webster was sure that the plot had elements that could be enhanced by good direction and sensitive camera work.

But Hildreth was always with him; on the patio and the beach; in the living room at night with the radio turned on, and every night before they went to bed she drove him as far as Monaco, and once to Menton where they talked with the Italian border guards.

On the beach one afternoon as he was writing, she said, "I don't know about French divorce laws but I don't see how Frederic can get any of my money."

"He'll probably try."

"Why should he? He's got his own money now. He made it by using mine. I think he just ought to let me go without making any trouble."

"Were you married in the Church?"

She shook her head. "There's no problem about that. It's just that I don't want him to have anything that should belong to you."

"He won't."

She rolled over on her side to face him and touched his notebook. "You'll only have to work when you want to, darling. Not all the time, like now."

Webster looked at her, and said, "Leave me a little pride, Hil. I'm not marrying you for your money. We're going to be married because it's probably the best thing for both of us."

She said, "For a while we probably can't live only on what you earn."

"In time I'll get my money back from the picture and I'll keep on writing. I'll sell things again."

"I know; but I won't want you to feel peculiar about using our money for a while."

"I'll hope we won't have to."

She rolled onto her back and pulled off her bandeau. Her breasts looked like serpents coiled to spring. She said, "Everything will work out, darling. The way I feel about you, it can't happen any other way."

That night he wrote in the living room, and after a while, Hildreth got up from the sofa, and said, "I'm tired of just sitting here and drinking. Let's take a drive."

"Half an hour," he said. "I've got to a place where I have to think things through."

"An hour ago you said you were almost finished for tonight."

"I was too optimistic." He wet the point of the pencil with his tongue and looked at the sheets of handwritten manuscript lying on the top of the table. She had been drinking and he knew that she was restless again.

She came behind him and rested her hands on his shoulders. "Tell me about the story you're writing."

"It's still an outline, Hil. Ideas for characters, scenes and camera shots. When I make it into a screenplay you'll see it."

"I'd think you'd be able to pay a little more attention to me. We'll only be here another few days."

"I know."

She said, crossly, "Why do you have to spoil it all now, darling. Can't you do this work back in Paris?"

"I can. But I seem to remember you suggesting I do a little work while I was here."

"A little work, yes. Not days and days of it."

"It hasn't been that," he said. "Can't you go down to the beach? Do I have to be there all the time?"

He felt her fingers in the flesh of his shoulders. She said, "I want you to be. Remembering what we've done there excites me. Then I start wanting you. I come back hoping for a little attention, and you couldn't care less."

"You're always in heat," he told her. "You ought to do something about it."

"I need you to do it. I can't help the way I am."

He felt her body pressing against his back, and he thought, no, I guess you can't. Not the way you're made. You could do without food and water but you have to have it. You don't need jut one man; you need relays. He said, "I'm almost through with it, Hil. Go make yourself a drink or read in bed. When I've finished we'll do it all night."

She said, "Not then; now."

"No."

"What am I supposed to do with myself?"

He made a suggestion.

She said, "I've outgrown that. It never was very much fun."

"Then do something else."

"I will. I'll take a little drive. I'll be back later."

He felt her hands leave his shoulders, and as he turned he saw her walk out of the room. He lighted a cigarette and heard the Lancia engine start, then the grating of gravel under the tires as she turned the car and drove it up the little road.

In another hour he had finished the story outline, and as he gathered the sheets together he realized he ought to have them typed in Paris. Maybe Hélène could do that much. Because he was used to typing, the work had taken longer because it had to be written by hand. He should have brought his portable when he came.

On the terrace he smoked another cigarette and thought about the story again. So far it was only a framework, but there was no point in doing much more until he knew how much money there would be for location work and extras. Since the letter from Roland he had not heard from him again, and he wondered whether the picture would ever really be made, or whether, like so many other things, it would turn out to be something on which he had wasted both time and hope.

Before he got into bed he made a highball and drank it, wondering where Hildreth could be; feeling a little that if she had an accident he would be responsible. But then he thought, she's a big girl now, and she has to take some responsibility for what she does.

Finally he turned out the light and lay back on the pillow and went to sleep.

The sound of the Lancia engine in the driveway wakened him. Subconsciously he had been expecting to hear it, and so he did not waken completely. He heard it stop, and then the opening of the car door, and he thought that in a few minutes she would be in the bed beside him.

But later he woke again, realzing that she had not come into the bedroom, and he wondered if she had got drunk and passed out on the living room sofa. He remembered hearing her get out of the car, so at first he did not go outside. He put on slippers and walked into the dark living room, but in the moonlight, the sofa was empty. He opened the door and walked out to the terrace, thinking she might have fallen asleep on the sun lounge, but she was not there, either.

As he woke fully, it came to him that she might have decided to go swimming, and if she were drunk it would have been a bad thing to do. He began running down the path through the garden, and when he was beyond the shrubbery he could see the beach, and under the clear moonlight he could see Hildreth.

She was leaning back on her arms in the sand and her naked thighs were raised a little. There was a man on the sand with her and Webster could see what the man was doing. Her eyes were closed and he could hear her moan a little as she said something to the man.

There was no tenderness in what they were doing; no love-making. It was coarse, animal eroticism and it stabbed his belly like a bayonet. He walked into the moonlight and on the sand his feet made no noise, so that he was standing beside them watching her face as the man looked up. He saw Webster and crawled back quickly from Hildreth. In the moonlight his face was white and there was sweat on his forehead. Hildreth opened her eyes and saw Webster. She screamed.

As the man tried to get to his knees, Webster kicked him. He cried out in pain and fell back on the sand. He tried to get up again, but Webster kicked his heel against the man's face. The man fell backward and lay gasping.

He turned to look at Hildreth, and saw that she had not moved. Only her knees were down now, and her skirt covered her thighs. He called her a name.

She said, "What did you have to do that for? He wasn't doing anything to you."

He called her a name again.

She said, "He's only a boy. He wanted to make love to me, so I let him, and now you've hurt him."

"That wasn't making love. Not what you had him do. Love isn't anything like that." He walked over to where the man lay and turned his body so that he could see his face. It was a dark face and young. About nineteen, Webster thought. The boy had long sideburns like a Niçois fisherman, and his breathing came in quick spurts.

Hildreth said, "Don't hurt him any more. Please, Web." She had raised her right hand in front of her mouth as though to protect herself from him.

"All right," he said. "All right. That's enough. That's too much." He felt himself shaking with rage and disgust. He said, "I told you what you are. When I'm gone you can do anything you want."

She moved forward onto her knees and held out her hands toward him. "You can't go away," she pleaded. "Not after all we've had together. We're going to be married."

He looked at her face turned toward the moonlight, and saw that it was streaked with tears. She was crying, silently, and the way her body swayed he knew that she was half-drunk. He said, "I pity you." He turned and began walking away from her but she ran after him, her bare feet kicking the sand behind her, and she put her arms around his body. "No, Web. No. Not ever. Don't go. I didn't know what I was doing. I needed you and you wouldn't do anything about it. You didn't care about me. But I was wrong. I shouldn't have picked him up and brought him here. I only did it to get even with you."

"You are," he said, and shook away her arms. "You're even with me."

"Web," she called after him. "Web. Please don't go. I'll make everything all right. I promise I will. You can write and I won't bother you and I'll let you do anything you want with me." She began to sob hysterically.

"I've done everything I want with you," he said, and walked up the path into the garden, and to the house, thinking, a nymph. She turned out to be a nymph, after all, and I never realized it. I didn't realize she had a problem like that. I never knew.

He was still trembling as he packed his bags and when he carried them outside the house he looked down toward the beach again, but he could not see them and there was no sound of voices—not even of a woman crying.

Carrying his bags, he walked up the road toward Eze, and when he reached a street-light he turned one of the bags on end and sat on it, waiting for a *rapide* that would take him into Nice.

Riding in the rear of the bus, Webster took out a cigarette and lighted it, noticing that his hands were steady again. The other passengers were a waiter, two French sailors, a young girl in a party dress and an old man with a limp mustache. The waiter was sleeping, the sailors were looking out of the window toward the harbor, the old man read a syndicalist magazine, and the girl stared at the road ahead. Her hands held a crushed corsage.

The smoke in his lungs seemed to nourish him and he began to feel better. He felt well enough to realize he could have had a few drinks at the house before leaving, when now, after four in the morning, the possibilities of finding a drink in Nice would be very thin. *As* he smoked he began to wonder why he had left the house at all when he could have stayed comfortably in bed and left in the morning. She was the one who should have left, the wrong-doer.

But he had always known she was a bitch and worse. He had known what she was and any surprise about it now was only a fiction to bolster his pride. Remembering the beach made his stomach turn over. He looked out of the window at the dark hillside and tried to forget it.

Forget it, he told himself. Forget her. You hurt the boy when it was yourself you should have hurt. You're as bad as she is because for months you've helped her become what she is. You let yourself be kidded into thinking the month with her would be good for you, when it was only an excuse to do all the time what you did in Paris only occasionally and in a controlled way.

Not again, he said half-aloud. Not again with her or anyone like her. She doesn't know when to stop. She'll kill herself that way or someone will kill her because of what she is. He thought, I wonder if her husband ever found out. I wonder if he really knows what he's married to? Even a Frenchman wouldn't want that twenty-four hours a day, three hundred and sixty-five days a year, including Sundays and holidays. If he knows, he wouldn't want to admit it. Not to anyone. Not even to her. If she didn't know before, she knows now, and in the morning when she looks into the mirror she'll see herself and she'll know. For the first time, really.

He flicked ash from his cigarette, and thought, something must have happened to her between Evanston and here. Or maybe only because of tonight and the drinking. It could have been just that. But I acted like an outraged husband and kicked the boy senseless when he had the least to do with it of anyone. The least. Really. It wasn't him or who he was, because he was only a symbol of what we've all become, and when I left it wasn't that I couldn't stand the sight of her, Hildreth—Hildreth Kaufman—or the comfortable house, but because I had to stop living that kind of life, and the boy and Hil and the sickness on the beach was an excuse to let me do it without having to face the fact that I knew we should never get married. So it was easier to watch them and kick the boy and bloody his face and call her what I did, because it got me out of something that might never have ended if she'd come back to Paris, as she'll have to. Eventually.

But not so soon now, and not for the same reason, and she won't be coming up to old Web's flat any more, and without me she'll have a chance to stop being what every mirror from now on will tell her she is, and if she isn't too far gone, she'll get a divorce and be free to be whatever she wants. Alone.

Alone, he thought. And now, I'm alone, too. But because I want to be and have to be. Yes. For a long time, and until I've got my own problems solved I can't solve them with someone else. Not with Hil. Not ever again those easy-to-part loins and the seeking mouth and the lips that crush so willingly, and the body arching like a fine rod. No. Not again. Not ever Hil.

Because she's behind me now and with her a part of my life that had to be lived through, I suppose, before I could go on to another part of it that still has to be lived. She may even have felt that it was ending, and so tonight, because there was nothing to be lost, she did what she did, knowing that if it was not then it would be the next day or the day after, but always feeling finality ahead, and not wanting to recognize it, but still holding on, just a little longer: always clinging to what was still pleasant and exciting and accustomed.

Always the postponement, he thought. Both of us, when there was nothing between us but bed, as she said herself, and never could have been because she was a girl from Evanston with money and a rich French husband and a flame in her loins that not even the ocean could quench. And all, most likely because she hasn't ever found the happiness she was brought up to think she deserved, and the inadequate feeling that lovers and what they could do helped only for a while. But never for long enough. Not so long as the other thing was there.

I'm sorry about the boy, he thought, but he'll get over the pain and the shock, and maybe she'll let him make love to her before she leaves the Côte. She ought to do that for him, because he certainly wasn't getting anything out of it the other way. All he got was a kick in the face, and he was the most surprised fisherboy on the Côte when it happened. Either she never told him there was a man in the house, or else she got too drunk to care before they came to the beach, and when he wakes up tomorrow he'll have a hangover like he never had before, and he ought to start hating her guts.

I'm sorry for him, and I'm sorry for her. Really sorry. And I'm sorry for myself. I told her I pitied her, and that's what she'll remember about me; that I pitied her. She'll forget the good nights in bed and on the sofa and the beach and in the water and she'll remember only that much of it. The last. She'll never know the way I felt about myself. The way I feel now. The way I wish I could get up and walk away from myself now and never look back…

The *rapide* began to slow, and Webster realized that they were pulling into the station in Nice. It had been a long ride in the night with no one to talk to, and now they were in Nice that was asleep with only street-lights and the floodlights over the bus station and a few porters dozing on outside benches, and when the bus stopped, he pulled down his bags and carried them off the bus to a taxi and woke the driver to ask when the morning plane left for Paris.

10.

Unpacking in his bedroom, he tried to keep sand from falling on the floor, but it was in his shoes and his trunks and some fell on the floor where it would stay to remind him of the Côte. He got the story outline out of the bag and carried it into his living room. Taking some sheets of clean paper from a drawer he set up his portable typewriter and began to retype the story outline, making a carbon copy for himself.

By the time he had finished typing, it was evening. He went down to a restaurant and ate dinner. Then he went back up to his flat, rolled clean paper into his typewriter and began working again. He finished the story outline by midnight.

In the morning he separated all the sheets and clipped them together. Paul and Henri could always find someone who could write a full screenplay from his outline, but it would not be the same screenplay that he would write. If they wanted to hire him, he would do it, but if they did not, he would flesh it into a screen original and send it to the Coast.

Finishing the story outline gave him a feeling of confidence that he had not known in a long time. He thought, it shows I can do it when I really want to. When I have the time and the craving, I can do it, and I can do it again; often enough so I won't be the frightened man I was when Paul and Henri first put their claws into me. It's given me back my self-respect.

There was coffee enough in the kitchen to put into the percolator, and while it was boiling he separated dirty laundry from his coats and slacks and tied it up in a bundle with sheets and pillowcases. Then he drank the coffee black, because he had no cream or milk, and carried the laundry and the letter down to Raspail. The *concierge* sold him a stamp, and he mailed the letter in a corner box and took his laundry to the *blanchisserie.* The proprietress undid his bundle and counted each piece. She was a red-faced, middle-aged woman with bleached hands, and she said, "You have been patronizing another *blanchisserie?*"

"No. I've been away."

"*Bien.* You will stay now for a while in Paris?"

"Yes," he said. "I'll be here for a while." Steam drifted toward him from the rear of the shop and he could see a woman ironing, another washing shirts, and a third was mending at a table. The smell of soap was warm and clean and familiar. The *blanchisserie* had become part of his life in Paris, and he was glad he had come back to it. Before he left, he said, "No starch."

"I remember, *m'sieu. Sans amidon.*" She smiled and said, "In two days?"

"If you can." He went out of the shop and took a taxi to the Porte de Versailles where Roland Perrex lived.

As he rode across Paris, he noticed that the leaves were changing color, and that the afternoon was cooler than the afternoons a month ago. Otherwise, Paris had not changed. He had not expected it to change except for the fact that he had been away and forgotten it a little.

He knocked at Roland's door, and when there was no answer he tried it, but the door was locked. He knocked again, and then he heard Roland call, "Who is it?"

"Robert."

"Oh."

"Open up."

"Patience, *mon ami.*"

"I thought you wanted me to hurry back."

"*Oui.* But not without warning."

Webster wondered who was with Roland at this time of the afternoon. He rattled the door again, heard Roland curse him, and then the door was opened. Roland's hair was mussed and he looked tired. He said, "You will forgive me, but we were having tea and there was a crisis with the crockery."

Webster went into the room and saw a woman seated on the sofa. She was pretty and a little rumpled.

"Well," Roland said, "You were to meet her, anyway, Robert. This is Mademoiselle Suzette La Claire."

She rose from the sofa and gave Webster her hand. She said, "I have heard so much about you from Roland."

Webster said, "I didn't realize you'd started the picture already."

"Not quite yet." Roland said: "We were waiting, as a matter of course, for your return." He sounded nettled.

Suzette said, "I hope you 'ave written your story, Monsieur Robert."

"I've worked on it," Webster said.

She smiled, and Webster saw that her smile and her teeth were good. She would be attractive to a man like Frederic. Evidently she was also attractive to Roland. She said, "I should love to hear your story."

"Paul and Henri should hear it first," Webster said. "It is possible that they will not care for it."

"But I am sure they will. Roland has told me that you are a famous writer of films, and now that I have met you I know that it must be so." She turned toward Roland, and said, "I know so little of motion pictures that I try to learn as much as I can even before the picture begins."

"You're learning from an expert," Webster said. "Monsieur Perrex is a famous director. Under him you are bound to succeed."

Suzette looked at her wristwatch and said, "I must go to keep an appointment."

Roland said, "I will call you tomorrow, Suzette. Robert and I will be busy today with technical details."

She gave her hand to Webster again, and said, "I am happy to know you, *m'sieu,* and I will ask Roland to tell me your story when it has been agreed upon."

Webster watched her walk to the door, and then he went to the window and looked down at the street while Roland said goodbye to her. When the door closed, Roland turned to him, and said, "Buffoon, I suppose you will think that we are intimate, this child and I."

Webster said, "How about a cup of tea?"

"It is not precisely tea that we were making. She is a pretty thing, but clumsy. I have been endeavoring to show her something of our art."

Webster said, "She looks like a fast learner."

"She possesses an agile mind. The little pigeon and I had just reached an understanding."

Webster took his copy of the story outline from his pocket and handed it to Perrex. "You might look it over," he said. "If you feel like discussing art."

Perrex took the outline and sat down in a chair near the window. While he read, Webster made himself a drink and stood looking out over the rooftops of Paris. Finally Perrex put down the outline and looked up at Webster. He said, "*Mon ami, les macreaux* will be unable to resist it. Myself, I am charmed. Our Suzette is to play the part of Michele?"

Webster nodded. "Unless they insist on making her the star."

"No. I am sure they will not do that. Not this time."

"How about the cost?"

Perrex said, "When it comes to cutting costs, I am a magician. We should do the location work as soon as possible and before the winter comes. Then we go into the studio."

"How about the rest of the casting?"

"Only a detail," Perrex said. "They will leave that to me. And how long will you require to write the screenplay?"

"It depends on the contract. By the week it should take about three months. For a flat fee I can do it in three weeks."

Perrex said, "It is a workable story, Robert. Not extreme or fanciful, but something with which to work. It has a certain quality and I am glad that you did it. You will see Paul and Henri today?"

"Tomorrow."

"You should not wait. They are eager to see you. Let me tell them you are here."

"No."

"Frederic is a cautious man, *mon ami.* He has not simply arranged a credit for them to finance the entire picture. Instead, he gives them only enough each week to cover the immediate costs. That way he controls what they do."

"He's smarter than I thought."

"He is not emotional." Roland drank from his glass. "Please see them today."

"Not today. I didn't sleep well last night."

"The train was uncomfortable?"

He shook his head. "I came yesterday by plane."

Perrex got up and made himself a drink. He looked at Webster, and said, "The lady did not break her leg, by any chance?"

"No."

"You quarrelled with her?"

"Yes."

"I see."

Webster sat down and took back the outline from Perrex. "Sometime I'll tell you about it. Right now it's something I want to forget."

Perrex said, "Well, then, forget her." He looked at Webster. "I am sorry you are depressed."

"Everyone has something that depresses them. Even clowns."

"Particularly clowns. You know the story about Grock?"

"Everyone knows it."

"Yes. It has a deep moral. Very likely he was in love and unhappy; otherwise he would have been able to overcome his depression."

Webster nodded.

Perrex said, "You are comparatively well off, *mon ami.* At least you did not marry her. Once I married an Englishwoman. It was during the war and we mistook patriotism for passion."

"That was a general mistake."

Perrex got out his black address book, and said, "Before I, too, become depressed let me suggest that we instigate a festival tonight."

"I don't feel like it."

"Very well, we will remove it from consideration." He looked at Webster. "You are very pure today. It is an unusual effect for the Côte. Almost unheard of."

Webster did not say anything.

"While you were gone, my friend, I was oppressed with uncertainties. Cultivating Suzette was a way to keep myself occupied until your return." He pointed to the outline, and said, "You will see our friends tomorrow, without fail?"

Webster nodded.

"*Tiens.* If we are to get drunk I must buy more whiskey. Of late I have drunk tea almost exclusively."

"There isn't a tea leaf in the place."

"Shall I procure a new bottle for a limited celebration?"

"Wait until after the picture before we celebrate."

"As you wish. But it is a beautiful day. We ought to take a fiacre through the Bois. From now on the beautiful days are numbered."

"They're always numbered," Webster said. "There's the same number every year, only each year goes faster than the last."

"It was an excellent summer," Perrex said. "Except for the unpleasantness with Paul and Henri. Otherwise, quite remarkably excellent."

"I didn't notice," Webster said. "I had those two bastards on my mind and Hil and another woman, and that's how the summer was for me."

"They did not ruin the summer for me entirely. I have some pleasant memories."

"Except for the war it was the worst summer I ever knew."

"You will keep on living in Paris?"

"Why not?" He looked at the bottom of his empty glass.

"You have friends back in Hollywood."

"I had. So long as I could pick up checks and throw parties. But movie people can't afford the restaurants any more. All the restaurants get now is the oil and department store trade."

"And you would not like that atmosphere?"

"I'd hate it." He stood up, and said, "I'll call tomorrow and let you know what our producers say."

"Please. I will want to know." He walked to the door with Webster, and said, "As I think about it, the story improves. It will be a good picture to make."

"We'll see." He took the lift down to the street and a taxi drove him back to the Boulevard Raspail.

That evening he walked from Raspail to the Ile de la Cité and ate dinner in a restaurant behind Notre Dame. It was pleasant to watch the lights of barges moving slowly down the Seine, and the air was cool. The Ile gave him a sense of isolation from the rest of Paris, and later when the streetlights came on, Notre Dame was only a darker shadow against the darkening sky.

He walked along the Quai des Orfevres to the Pont Neuf and crossed onto the Rue Dauphine. A wind began to blow and it became damp and chill. He stopped at a *brasserie* to warm himself and had a *fine café*. The windows were steamed from the inside and the warmth and the good smell cheered him a little.

He lighted a cigarette and thought about Hildreth Kaufman. He wondered if she were in bed now with the Niçois and whether, for her, it had been a good exchange. He looked at the steamed windows of the *brasserie* and decided that Eze would be warm and comfortable and unlike Paris in October. Nice would be the same, and Cannes and Monaco and along the boulevards the palms that looked like inverted feather dusters would keep their greenness through the winter. And the sea would still be warm and the nights…

He said to himself, how close it was; how very close. And if it had happened after we were married I would have shot them on the beach and turned the barrel into my mouth and pulled the trigger again. Even if it proved nothing I think I might have done it that way.

He thought again of the Côte and wondered if Tay were there with Rino Menotti. Probably, he said to himself. Very probably they're already there, shacked up the way I was with Hil, and she'll watch him drive in the big race and then they'll have a banquet afterward with champagne in the big loving cups and she'll think all that's pretty immense. Well, let her think so; I won't be seeing her any more, nor Lydia nor Lee. I can find a life for myself in Paris that won't touch on any of theirs.

But I still feel lousy about Hildreth. Absolutely lousy; as though she'd made me eat *merde*. That's how I feel. She was too much of a good thing. Too much. And a good thing she was while it lasted, but with her it would be always just a question of time. That's all. Just time. And then it would be the gardener or the bellboy or Roland or Paul Gringold, or anyone who happened to be handy when she started to feel that way. It must be a terrible thing to be the way she is; to know it's coming over you and not be able to fight it at all. And later, not even to want to fight it because what's so necessary is so easy to have.

"She'll probably never divorce Frederic now. She'll have her lovers and he'll have Suzette and others after her, and so that's how it will be for them. Not a pleasant life, he thought. Not a happy life for either one. So I was lucky to find out when I did. Luckier than I deserve.

He paid for his coffee and walked out to the street again. There were no stars in the sky and the wind had become very cold. From now on he would have to begin wearing a topcoat.

The next day he had lunch with Kress and Gringold in their George V suite, and when the waiter had wheeled away the service cart, Gringold said, "Well, Web, how about it? Got anything for us?"

Webster took the story outline from his pocket. "I've done some work on the screenplay," he said.

"Good fellow." Gringold rubbed his hands together. "I knew you'd do it; you wouldn't let us down."

Webster did not move to give Gringold the outline. Instead, he said, "There's about a thousand dollars outstanding between us, Paul. How do we stand on that?"

"Hell, everything's gonna work out; just don't worry about it. Let me do your worrying for you."

"That's not worth a damn, Paul."

"Why, Web. What's the matter?"

"Oh, Christ," Webster said. "I thought we were going to talk facts today. I don't care if you buy the story or not. But if you want to read it you'll have to pay what you owe me."

Gringold said, "Money's been awfully tight." He stirred uncomfortably.

"We made an agreement."

"I guess we did. But you know the sort of things you run up against in this business."

"Sure. And you and Henri are two of the things I've run up against." He put away the outline, and stood up. "It was a good lunch," he said. "But because you've been eating so well all along you've lost touch with reality. You seriously expect me to laugh off a thousand dollars and hand you a screenplay so you can get your production started." He shook his head. "Get someone else." He looked at Henri Kress, and said, "*Bon jour. Avec toutes mes compliments.*"

Kress stood up quickly. "Do not be unreasonable, Monsieur Robert. Because we 'ave been engulfed in a t'ousand details, the matter of your money 'as slipped our minds."

"Too bad," Webster said, "because this is a good story."

"How do you know?" Gringold asked.

"Perrex read it; he says so." Webster took out a cigarette and lighted it. "I don't think you two are really producers at all. Other producers I worked for had talent to add to a film, or money enough to hire people with talent. You haven't either talent or money."

Gringold stood up. "What are you going to do with the story?"

"Sell it," Webster said. "There's always a buyer for a good story. I'll probably do better with another producer."

Henri Kress looked at Paul Gringold, and then he took out his billfold and slowly counted out ten, one-hundred dollar bills. He handed them to Webster. "We were going to use this for somet'ing else, Monsieur Robert, but today the story is the mos' important t'ing."

Webster looked at the money and put it in his billfold. "All right," he said. "Here's the story. Read it and make up your minds if you want it."

Gringold took the story from him and walked toward the window. He sat down in a chair and began to read. Webster gave the carbon copy to Kress. He said, "I'll be back in an hour."

He went out of the room, walked down to the lobby of the hotel and sat at the bar deciding what his terms would be. If they were not acceptable to the two men he would have to try to make other arrangements; with someone else.

Looking around the barroom he saw couples at tables, talking together, and he felt a little lonely. He thought of Tay Crandall who was probably on the Riviera with her Italian, and he decided that the sooner he began to work again the better it would be. He wanted to work hard each day and night for as long as it took to make the picture. That way he would feel less lonely. While he had been making the last picture he had met Hildreth Kaufman; perhaps he woud meet some one else this time. Only not someone like Hil. Someone different.

Like Tay, he thought. Someone like her is what I really want, but since it isn't to be Tay it'll have to be someone else. Only where will I find someone like her?

He decided that when the picture was made he would go down to Italy for a while. He had not been there since the war, and he had never seen Venice and the Lido. Or if the picture were finished by March there would still be time to ski in the Arlberg or possibly at Davos. In June he could go to Majorca and write again. That way he would keep busy.

When he had been at the bar for an hour he walked back up to the suite and opened the door. The partners were talking, and when they saw him, Paul said. "You've really done it, Web. You've got a great picture here."

"Want it?"

"Hell, yes."

Webster walked toward them, and said. "You can have it for ten thousand dollars. Pay me in a week."

The partners looked at each other. Henri Kress said, "We cannot pay you so much, Monsieur Robert. Please, you must take less."

Webster sat down and looked up at them. "I'll take less," he said. "I'll even take nothing at all; but we'll have to make a change in the production staff."

"What do you mean?" Gringold said. "Like what, Web?"

"Put me in charge of production. Complete charge."

Gringold blanched. "I can't just do a thing like that."

"Why not? You want the story, and you can't pay for it. You've got to start turning cameras in two months and you know it. What will you do for a story?"

Gringold said, "What do you mean by complete charge of production?"

"You two can hire the cast and the technicians and run the production schedule. Perrex and I will handle the script and the direction. We'll edit the film and put it together. You won't come near the set."

Kress said, "You are serious?"

"Completely serious. We'll shoot each scene in French and in English. That'll mean a larger cast, but it'll give us a decent export market. You know what kind of business sub-titled films do; little theaters and foreign screenings. To hell with that. Make a good film in English and we'll have something that will make us some money."

"And what else do you want?" Kress asked.

"Ten percent of the profit after production costs have been absorbed. That makes it my gamble, too. You two want to be producers; all right. I'm giving you a chance to have your name on a good film. A film that'll be shown in the States, not just in Haute Alsace and Lugano."

Gringold took out a cigar, nicked the end of it with his thumbnail and lighted it. He said, "Web, you're a damn good screen writer, but you've never produced a picture before."

Kress said, "Monsieur Kaufman expects us to be the producers."

"You don't have to tell him you aren't. I don't care whether the screen credits calls me a writer or executive producer. What I want is a good picture. That's all I want."

"And ten percent," Gringold said, thoughtfully.

"If it's a good picture there'll be enough profit so you'll never notice my ten percent."

Kress said, “We ’ave made a different arrangement with Kaufman.”

“Then take five percent from each of your own percentages.” He looked at Gringold, and said, “Well, Paul?”

Gringold turned to Kress, and said, “I guess we’ll have to, Henri. The story’s everything he thinks it is. And Web knows all he needs to know about production.”

Finally, Kress said, “Very well. The papers will be ready tomorrow.”

Gringold said, “Okay, Web. But don’t you think shooting in two languages at once is a little tricky?”

“A little. But it’s a hell of a lot cheaper than making two films. It won’t cost much more in the long run than making sub-titles. Labor costs are low here, so we can do it. A good first-cameraman will cost you only twenty dollars a day in France against five times that in the States.”

Gringold said, “All right. But we’ll have to tell Frederic.”

“He ought to accept your judgment. He wants a good picture, too—he’s investing in Suzette.”

Gringold came over to him and they shook hands. “I’ll handle Kaufman. You still sweet on the wife?”

“No.”

“Okay. It’ll be easier then.”

Henri Kress shook hands with him, and said, “You will begin to do the screenplay at once?”

Webster nodded. “We’ve got two months,” he said. “You can begin casting from the outline.”

He walked down to the Avenue George V and crossed the Champs-Élysées to the Cygne office. Hélène gave him some letters. He sat down to read them. One was from Tay. It said:

> At first I thought you didn’t come to my party because you’d gone to the Côte, but finally Lydia told me that she’d told you about Rino, and what you said.

> Web, it wasn't something I could bring myself to tell you that night. But what I said about Lee was the way I felt then. Please don't think I didn't mean all that I said to you. I guess I just didn't say enough, but I couldn't explain everything.

The letter was dated three weeks before.

He dictated some replies to Hélène, and then he tore up the letters and threw them into a wastebasket.

Walking down the stairs he passed *Madame's* office but he did not go in. He went back to his flat and called Roland Perrex.

11.

AFTER THREE DAYS of working on the screenplay Webster had a night of considerable gaiety with Roland Perrex in a series of cabarets and bistros around Montmartre.

He woke in the morning, not realizing at first what had wakened him, and then he heard the door buzzer again. The way it rang told him it was the *concierge.* His wristwatch said that the time was after nine.

He sat up slowly, put on a bathrobe and began walking toward the door. The floor was cold and Riviera sand grated under his feet. When he opened the door, the *concierge* said, "The telephone, m'sieu."

"Take the message," he said. He was tired and hung over.

"*Oui,* m'sieu." She looked inside his flat, and said, "It is very cold today."

"I can feel it."

"You will want some coal or wood for burning?"

"I guess so."

"*Bien.* You shall have it. It is essential that you be comfortable here."

He closed the door and went back to bed because he felt badly and because there was no heat in the flat.

His mouth tasted like baked mud and his intestines were as tight as twisted wires. He closed his eyes, hoping that the pain of getting up would go away; but he had remained vertical too long. It was like the aftermath of a spinal anaesthetic, he thought; if you lay perfectly horizontal you never noticed it, but if you ignored the nurse and tried to sit up, the ceiling fell on your head and the pain stayed for a week.

He had not planned to get up this morning. He had no appointments to keep and nowhere to go. Not today. Not this afternoon or tomorrow or the next day.

Lying perfectly still he tried to concentrate on sleep, but the effort itself seemed to wake him and after a quarter of an hour he gave up. Perhaps the *concierge* would be able to arrange for the coal and wood today so that tomorrow he would not have the same problem. He tried to light a Bleu but his mouth rejected it, and he stubbed it out.

Walking to the bathroom, he tried to think who might have called him at nine o'clock in the morning. Anyone who knew him well would know he would not be likely to be awake. So someone who did not know him well must have called. Well, whoever it was could wait. Running cold water into the basin he lowered his face into it, feeling the shock like a physical blow. He sucked some of the water into his mouth, and then he came up to breathe and filled a glass under the tap and drank.

As he gave himself a cold sponge bath he decided that for the winter he ought to go to a hotel that catered to ladies of the street. Then there would be hot water all night and all day, and no trouble with the management about it. Even hot water from a *bidet* would be better than no hot water at all.

He shaved slowly and carefully with cold water, and while he was dressing he heard the *concierge* come into the living room. When he was dressed he found that a fire had been built in the living room stove and the room was beginning to warm. He put on a topcoat and walked down to Raspail for a breakfast of hot milk with chocolate and buttered *brioche*.

When Webster returned the *concierge* was filling out an account book. He went inside and the *concierge* handed him a torn sheet of paper. The name *Crandall* was written on it. She said, "It was the voice of an old woman."

"What did she want?"

"She asked that you come to see her this morning, m'sieu."

"Did she say why?"

"No. But I think that she wants to see you very much."

When he had first seen the name written by the *concierge,* he had thought it was Tay who had called him. But she would be on the Riviera by now; down there with her Italian.

The *concierge* said, "If you wish I will make the fire for you each morning."

"Yes," he said, and tipped her for the telephone message. Then he gave her five thousand francs for stove fuel and went up to his flat.

The living room was warm and as he looked at the typed pages lying on his coffee table, he decided that he ought to work again. To hell with Lydia and whatever she wanted to talk about. She should know that she could no longer consider him obligated to the Crandall family.

He lighted a cigarette and sat down in front of his typewriter. If he could work this way for another week he would have the screenplay finished; then he and Roland could begin solving the production problems.

He read what he had written yesterday, and he was a long time recalling the mood of the last scene but he forced everything else from his mind, and finally he began to type. Last night's liquor and the lack of sleep made him a little shaky, and after a while he went into the kitchen and made some coffee. He drank a cup and poured another to carry back to the living room.

Thinking of the next scene he would write, he walked toward the typewriter, and he had almost reached it before he realized that someone else was in the room. A woman was seated in a chair smoking a cigarette. He looked at her face and saw that the woman was Hildreth. She held out her hand, and said, "I'll take the coffee before you spill it. I suppose you made it for me, darling."

He said, "I never expected to see you again."

She uncrossed her legs and slipped out of her fur coat. "You're very foolish to have thought such a thing. Because I was a trifle gregarious at Eze is really no reason for us to stop seeing each other." She looked at him through the smoke of her cigarette. "Is it?"

"It's one of the best reasons in the world," he said, and put down the coffee beside his typewriter.

"You seem to have accomplished some writing since we parted," she said, casually.

He said, "There's nothing between us anymore, Hil. Nothing. I'm trying to work, so please go away."

She laughed silkily. "You're so very sweet, darling—wanting to protect your pride and your professional armor—but you know perfectly well there'll always be something between us. Until one or the other of us is dead."

He shook his head. "You're wrong."

"No I'm not."

He said, "You've never been so wrong, Hil. You know what you are. Do you expect me just to forget it?"

"Why not? Husbands have, and we aren't even married. My God, you don't think the little interlude with that boy meant anything to me?"

"That's what's wrong," he said. "It didn't mean any more to you than brushing your teeth. But it meant something to me because I'd kidded myself into thinking we could make a go of marriage."

She leaned forward and stubbed out her cigarette. "Let's forget the marriage part," she said. "Let's even forget the love." She took off her gloves. "Forget everything, Web, except that we're two unusual people who are remarkably good for each other, and there's no reason why we shouldn't continue to be."

Beneath her low-cut jersey blouse her breasts seemed fuller than he had ever seen them before. There were dark crescents under her eyes. He said, "I'm so old-fashioned I won't share a woman."

"You'd never have to share me, Web."

He shrugged. "Maybe not today or next week, but eventually you'd duck into the broom closet with someone, and there'd be Eze all over again." He shook his head. "No, thanks, Hil. I'm cutting my losses while I can."

Her face hardened. "You can't refuse me."

"I have."

She said, "By whatever you hold holy, I'll swear I'd be faithful to you."

"Once you swore you'd be faithful to Frederic, but how long did that last?"

"To hell with Frederic." She kicked off her shoes and walked across the room to him. Kneeling she tried to kiss his lips. He turned his head away, and said, "Don't, Hil."

"I want you, Web. I want you now."

"No."

"I've got to have you." Her voice was insistent. "Haven't you any consideration for the way I feel?"

"No."

"You don't know how awful it is to want someone the way I want you."

"I don't want to know."

Her tone changed. Her voice wheedled. "Please, Web; just this once, then. I want you so much."

"Just go," he said. "I don't want to talk about it."

Finally she slipped on her shoes, and then she said, "You've found someone, haven't you? You're in love with someone else."

"I'm just not in love with you. I'm sorry for you, Hil. I've said that before. There are places in Switzerland that treat what you've got. You ought to go to one of them before it's too late."

"What do you mean?"

"You know what I mean."

She looked at him then and she began to cry. "Yes, I know, and I'm afraid. I know what happens, but I've got to have you now." She tried to put her arms around him.

"Don't make it worse. Find someone else."

"I want you. I don't want anyone else."

He stood up and looked down at her, crouching like an animal in front of his feet. "I said no."

She turned her eyes upward, and said, "All right, you bastard. I'll tell you a better reason why we're starting over again."

"Tell me."

Her lips curled a little as she spoke. "You're writing a screenplay for my husband. One word from me would stop all that. Then you'd never have your picture—the picture you want and need." She caught his hands and pulled herself to her feet. "The way I need you." Her body moved against him and she clawed his hips with her fingers.

He said, "You slut, do you think you can force me to make love to you?"

Her answer came in a rush of words. "I know what you want. I know for you a good picture is the most important thing in the world, but for me, right now, having you is the most important thing in the world." Her lips brushed the hollow of his throat. "You could have both, Web. It's so easy. So terribly easy."

"So easy," he said. "Yes, it's always been so easy, Hil. You've been too easy and that's why it's all over."

Her voice rose. "I'll tell Frederic about Eze and he'll stop the picture."

Webster laughed. "I imagine he knows about you by now." He walked past her, picked up her coat and threw it at her. It caught across her shoulder. He said, "Tell your husband anything you want. Let him stop the picture if he wants to."

"He'll stop it. He'll turn it off like a faucet. He'll ruin you because I'll tell him to do it."

"You'll like that, won't you?"

"I'll *love* it," she said, viciously. "I'll love seeing your dreams destroyed." Her voice rose steadily in a weird, off-key progression. "You'll be broke, finished, starving to death by the time I've finished with you. Then you'll come crawling back to me. Who were you to call me a whore? Who were you to judge what I did?"

"I'm not judging you," he said, fiercely. "But I've had enough of you. For a while I thought there was a chance for you—for both of us—but there never was. You don't attract me now; you sicken me with your rottenness—with the private sickness you call love. You're diseased, Hil. Recognize it, for God's sake."

"Shut up," she shrieked at him, hysterically. "Damn you. Shut up, shut up, *shut up!*"

He picked her up suddenly, and carried her twisting and struggling to the door. He set down her feet in the corridor, but her legs were kicking and she stumbled against the railing, the coat falling from her shoulders. As her body struggled awkwardly to push itself upright, he saw the twisted seams of her stockings, the disarrayed hair, the red gash of her contorted mouth and the hatred in her eyes.

She spat at him.

He wiped the spittle from his face with the palm of his hand and then he turned from her and closed the door, shutting her outside his room.

Weak, sickened by her hysteria and his own revulsion he leaned back against the door and closed his eyes. He thought he heard her weeping outside the door and finally her footsteps moved away and the stairway creaked as it took her descending weight.

He went back to the typewriter and picked up the cup of coffee, but his hands were trembling and the cup had lost most of its warmth. Instead, he lighted a cigarette and tried to read the sheet he had been typing. As he read he realized that until he could forget her he would not be able to work. Memories better forgotten had flared upward like flames licking from coals that had been fanned by an unexpected wind.

He put on his coat and walked down the stirway to the Boulevard Raspail. The sunshine made the day seem less cold and the clear air was good in his lungs. By the time he had walked to the Seine he felt that he was under control again.

Near a bookstall he leaned against the railing and looked across the river to the Place de la Concorde. He could see the Obelisk and the Crillon, the gray façade of the Rue de Rivoli, and stretching away to the left the tree-lined borders of the Champs-Élysées. Over there were the Cygne offices and in the same building the offices where Tay worked. He felt a sudden compulsion to go there and talk with her if only to wash Hildreth Kaufman from his mind, but Tay would have left Paris by now for the Riviera and the *Rallye* with Rino Menotti.

At last the thing with Hildreth was over; finished, finally, because it had run its course. It was over and she was gone and he would never see her again.

As he watched the surface of the Seine he felt isolated and completely alone. The feeling began to grip him more strongly until he took a deep breath of the cold air and began to walk along the embankment toward the Ile St.-Louis.

Frederic Kaufman sat behind his desk and stared unbelievingly at his wife. She looks like a maniac, he thought. Or else she's drunk coming here like this, running red-faced through the reception room and letting the clerks and typists see her the way she looks.

He stood up, slowly, and said, "Is it reasonable to come here as you are, my dear? Important clients might see you; what would they think?"

Hildreth Kaufman dropped her coat across the arms of a chair and placed her hands on his desk. Looking across the width of the desk at her husband's face, she said, unsteadily, "*Merde* on what they think—what anyone thinks. We haven't seen each other in a long time, Frederic. Is that how you greet me?"

He looked down at the polished surface of his desk. It was Circassian walnut burnished to a mirror-like finish. He could see the ends of his moustache twitching. He looked up, and said, "But you give me no warning, my dear. You had but to let me know you were once more in Paris. Instead, you burst in upon me like a madwoman and seem to expect a maximum of deferential treatment."

"I deserve it—I'm your wife."

He held up one hand. "Let us say rather that we are married. This past month I have been forced to speculate on just whose wife you really are."

"I'm still your wife, darling. Believe me, I'll never leave you again." She tried to make her words sound sincere.

He raised his eyes slowly to look at her puffed, unlovely face. "Is that by way of a threat, Hildreth? I fancy that too much compatibility could become as tiresome as too little."

"Don't be clever, Frederic," she said, sullenly. "I'm not in the mood for it. Spare me your cleverness." She ran one hand through her tangled hair, opened her bag and took out a cigarette. She waited for Frederic to light it, but he stepped back from the desk to the corner cellarette and opened the top. From the refrigerator section he lifted a split of Pommery. "Will you join me?" he asked.

"Of course." She lifted the desk lighter and pressed the spring lever. A jet of ignited gas sprang outward and her lips lowered the tip of her cigarette into its steady flame. She saw her husband peel off the bottle's metallic wrapping, twist open the wire retainer and work the cork out of the bottle. The pop was amplified in the large quiet office.

Frederic took two champagne glasses from the cellarette and set them on the desk. While he poured champagne into them Hildreth exhaled smoke toward the window that overlooked the Place Vendôme. She could see people walking up the stairway into the Ritz. A fiacre stopped at the entrance and the doorman helped two old women descend.

Frederic walked around the side of his desk and handed his wife a glass of champagne. "We should have a toast," he said, "after so long a parting. Shall it be to Love?"

"No. Just to us. To you and me." She lifted her glass, tilted it and drank deeply. "I never should have gone to the Riviera, Frederic. I was a fool ever to leave."

"If you will permit me to say so, I found your departure a trifle impulsive."

"Is that all you have to say?"

He shrugged. "From your tone, from your expression, I judge that you managed to make a fool of yourself."

"Damn you, I did. I was weak, darling; terribly weak. I went away with another man—at his insistence. I know I shouldn't have done what I did, darling, but you'd been ignoring me terribly. You were always occupied with Suzette."

"The man was … cruel to you, *chèrie?*"

"Terribly cruel, Frederic. He humiliated me. And at the end he laughed at you and mocked you." She tilted her glass again, sipping the golden fluid so that she could watch his face.

He said, "Now that your idyll is over, would you mind telling me whom you permitted to dishonor me?"

She put her hand on his wrist and said, "I made a bad bargain, darling. It was a terrible mistake. But try not to hate me; please try to understand."

His face did not change expression. "Who was it, Hildreth?"

She turned from him and fixed her eyes on one of the provincial prints on his wall. "Robert Webster," she said.

"I thought it would be Webster," he said, quietly. "His associate, Perrex, has taken a fancy to Suzette. Really, those two are an intolerable pair."

Puzzled by his bland voice, she turned, and said, "Well, what are you going to do about it?"

Frederic lifted the bottle of champagne and divided its contents between their glasses. He lifted Hildreth's glass to her hands and said, "Is some sort of action indicated, *chèrie?* Do you envision something as appallingly stylized as pistols in the Bois at dawn?" He sipped from his glass and looked reflectively out of the window at the tall Colonne that had been cast from the cannons of Napoleon's enemies. "Frankly, I have little stomach for such a prospect."

She said, "Don't you care, Frederic? Doesn't what's happened mean anything to you?"

"It might," he said, turning his eyes from the window. "It would depend upon your motives. For instance, why do you come here so hurriedly, so eager to confess your transgressions? Is it to anger me, to fill me with hatred? That is scarcely the action of the normal wife."

She said, "I sickened of him, Frederic. Even though he made love to me I could not bear to hear him mock you. 'A pompous little Parisian' he called you—a capon.' "

A spot of white appeared on each of Frederic's cheeks. "A capon, am I?" he said, half-aloud. "Cuckold, yes; capon, no." He finished his champagne quickly and put down the empty glass. He rubbed his hands together as though they were stiff with cold, and said, "Where is he now, this Robert of yours whom you now resent?"

"Here in Paris again."

Frederic Kaufman turned and walked around the end of his desk. He sat down in his chair and looked up at his wife. For a long time he said nothing, and when he spoke, he said, "You are a very beautiful woman and your body is capable of electrifying excesses. But your mind is devious, Hildreth, and although everything you have chosen to tell me is thoroughly plausible I do not necessarily believe any of it. In fact, both of us know you to be an accomplished liar and I would venture a large sum of money that you have lied to me once more."

She sneered at him. "I went away with Robert Webster. Do you need to see his fingerprints on my body?"

"That much I believe. As for the rest, it makes no real difference; except that for reasons of your own you told it to me, instead of concealing it."

"What kind of man are you? Doesn't it make a difference to you that I've slept with Robert Webster."

Frederic Kaufman shrugged. "You slept with him frequently in Paris. Is it greatly different that you slept together on the Riviera?"

She turned and threw her champagne glass against the wall. It broke on the frame of a print and the fragments fell down onto the carpeting. "Do something," she said in a fury. "He exists on your money. Are you so much of a coward that you will pay a man who makes love to your wife?"

Calmly her husband said, "I have paid him for professional services that did not include making love to you. That was your idea or his—or you decided upon it together. There is no relationship between the two things."

Her fists pounded his desk. *"Get rid of him!* Call Kress and Gringold and tell them he's through. Tell them to get rid of him. Make him sorry he called you a capon. Show him you're a *man.* My God, *do something!"*

He sat forward, leaned his elbows on the desk and looked upward into his wife's contorted face. "Control yourself, Hildreth. You must remember that a significant sum of money is invested in a production which Henri and Paul are to make with Robert Webster's assistance. Without him the two of them are helpless as jellyfish on a beach." He spread his hands explanatorily. "If I were to do what you desire I would be, in effect, punishing myself."

"I thought you loved me." Her voice had an uncomprehending quality.

"I am sure that once I loved you just as much as you must have loved me. But we have been married much too long to place any dependence whatever on that transitory sentiment. We will continue as man and wife because we are enough alike to see in each other a reflection of ourselves, and because the inertia of marriage is difficult to overcome. Believe me, the courts of France habitually make divorce as unpleasant as murder." He folded his hands in a clerical gesture.

"I thought you cared enough to want me for yourself—without sharing me with anyone else. My God, Frederic, are you content to see Webster go along smug and contented, knowing what he's been to me?"

He stared at his wife for a long time. Then he licked his lips, and said, "I am not averse to revenging myself upon Robert Webster, Hildreth, but only if the cost is not great."

"You place a price on your honor?" she asked.

"I did so long ago. I did so in my youth when I abandoned my first love and went to the United States to seek a wealthy wife. From the day I turned her away in tears I could lay no further claim to personal integrity." He looked at her disarrayed hair, at her lips drawn back in a sardonic smile, and finally he said, "What you ask me to do would cause the loss of all the money I have invested in the new film, and in addition the loss of prospective future profits. For despite your present differences with Robert Webster, the fact is that his story and his talents would make this an excellent and profitable film."

She said, "You're no patron of the arts, Frederic. Do what I say: call Henri Kress and have him get rid of Robert Webster."

He smiled regretfully and shook his head slowly. "That is a very insufficient excuse, my dear, but the proposition may not be altogether unworkable." He tapped his fingers on the desk judicially. "If you meet two requirements I will do as you ask."

She wet her lips. "What are they? What must I do?"

"Tell me the truth," he said. "Not even your holiest oaths could convince me that you and Webster parted merely because you could not bear to hear him ridicule your husband." His hands reached across the desk until they held her wrists, absorbing the heat of her flesh. "Tell me the truth, Hildreth," he said. "Tell me what happened to make you hate him."

She tried to draw away her wrists, but his grasp was firm. Her lips twisted into a sneer. "I'll tell you, then," she said. "I'll really tell you, you pompous little capon—I fell in love with Robert Webster while we were together at Eze and I asked him to marry me." Her face was intense, the muscles of her throat rigid.

Frederic Kaufman released his wife's wrists. He looked down at his buffed fingernails and pursed his lips carefully. "How very like you," he said. "And how interestingly told." He looked up to meet his wife's eyes. "Anger makes you astonishingly vibrant, my dear. Is it symptomatic of new reaches of passion you were able to discover with Webster?"

"Perhaps," she said, casually. "But you require the entire truth, Frederic."

"Continue," he said. "By all means spare nothing."

"I would have divorced you for Robert Webster," she snapped her fingers, "like that. But he discovered me in a compromising situation and left me."

"Highly commendable on his part," Frederic Kaufman said. "Wisely he considered the compromise a significant straw in the wind."

"I'm telling you everything," she said, and her words were rushed. "I couldn't let it rest at that, Frederic. He was in my blood, in my brain; the taste of his mouth was always in mine. Because I was insane to get back what I had lost by being indiscreet I went to his room a little while ago." She turned her face toward the window so that she would not have to watch her husband's eyes.

"I surmised as much," he said. "And what did your moralistic compatriot do?"

"He threw me out," she said, her facial muscles moving like wires. "He threw me out on my ass." She turned so that she could see her husband again. "I wasn't good enough for him."

"Evidently not."

"But I'm still good enough for you," she said, aggressively. "After a thing like that I can always come back to you. Because the only thing that matters to me is that he threw me out when I wanted him. That's what I'll never forget; that's what I'll never be able to forgive. That's why I'll do anything necessary to destroy him."

"Anything?" Frederic asked. "Hildreth, you really must temper your hatred with rationality."

"I hate him," she said, gutturally. "Tell me what else I must do. Tell me, Frederic."

He smiled until his lips parted, and he said, "You will help me repay Suzette for her indiscretions with Roland Perrex. The two of them—Webster and Perrex—have become intolerably troublesome to me, and so I am willing to terminate their services; very willing, Hildreth. There is only the matter of the money—the investment that was made in the enterprise."

"Write it off," she said. "It was a bad investment."

He shook his head. "My principals are notably unenthusiastic about bad investments, and withdrawing money at this time from something so promising would be, in a financial sense, indefensible. There would be no way by which I could ever make a satisfactory explanation."

"It *has* to be stopped, though," she said. "He has to suffer."

He nodded in agreement. "Exactly, my dear. And this is how you may achieve your desire in a way satisfactory to me: simply repay me for what has been expended on the enterprise to date."

She moved away from the desk and looked down through the window at the Place Vendôme where people were walking now that the working day had almost ended. She looked at the spiral bas-relief of the Colonne and tried to make out the endlessly ascending figures.

Turning back to her husband, she asked, "How much would it cost me?"

"I am not an accountant, Hildreth. It will take a few days to learn the exact figure."

"Roughly," she said.

He shrugged. "Nothing excessive—somewhere in the neighborhood of fifteen thousand dollars."

Her lips twisted. "I'll pay it," she said, and walked toward her husband's desk. "Do you want a check now?"

He waved his hand magnanimously. "It is not necessary at this time."

She opened a cigarette box, took out a cigarette and waited for him to press the lever of the butane lighter. She exhaled smoke toward the window, and said, "I'm so glad you've no duels scheduled this week, dear; you'd expect me to fight them for you, too."

His eyes held her as he lighted a cigarette for himself. "You did not marry an American like Robert Webster," he said. "Never forget that, Hildreth. You married me. By now you must have learned that European husbands are different."

"Different . . ." she echoed, bitterly. "My *God,* how different."

He was dialing a telephone number, and when he heard the voice of Hélène he asked for Henri Kress.

Hildreth Kaufman listened to what her husband was saying and felt herself suddenly go limp. She leaned heavily against the desk and her body began to glow with sensations of triumph and satisfaction.

After the way Robert Webster had rejected her she had thought she could never feel that way again.

Robert Webster walked up the stairs to his room, unlocked the door and took off his coat. His face was cold and he rubbed his hands together to warm them. Flexing his fingers he lighted a cigarette and sat down at his typewriter. The long walk along the Seine had cleared his mind of Hildreth Kaufman, and as he walked back along the embankment he had been able to plan part of his writing.

Putting a clean sheet of paper behind the roller of his typewriter he turned it into position and glanced at the last page he had typed. But before he began to type again he remembered the message that Lydia Crandall had called him. He took his hands away from the keyboard and blew smoke at the typewriter. For a moment he wondered what she could want from him, and then the thought was born that Tay might be in trouble.

As he thought about it, the possibility enlarged until he got up from his chair and went to the window. Looking down at Raspail he wondered what kind of trouble she could have that her money couldn't take away. If she's getting a big belly from Menotti her money will be a big help getting rid of it.

He thought, I haven't let myself think of it because it's nothing I wanted to flay myself with, but I didn't want Tay to be the way I found her. I wanted her to be Lee's kid sister—young and innocent—not the hard little pushover who'd slept around New York and Paris and didn't even hold out for love. His hand forced the cigarette between his lips again and he made himself fill his lungs with smoke. He exhaled, and thought, but what right have I to hope for anything like that? After the things I've done ... after the life I've lived ... after Hildreth ...

Turning from the window he began walking toward the typewriter, knowing that he would have to begin writing quickly or he would be lost in memories and conjectures for the rest of the evening. But the door opened behind him and as he turned quickly, he saw Roland Perrex. His friend's face was red with cold and he was panting with exertion. Perrex said, "Give me a drink, Robert." He gasped for air. "I need one badly."

Webster went to the kitchen, splashed Scotch into the bottom of a glass and brought it back to Perrex who was sitting in a chair staring up at the ceiling. Perrex took the whiskey from Webster and gulped it down. "My God," he said, "but we are unlucky, we too."

"I'm unlucky," Webster said, "but why you?"

"Because it is my misfortune to know you; it is my destruction that I am fond of you." He looked through the bottom of the glass at Webster, and said, "Ah, what a noble thing friendship is."

"It's wonderful," Webster said. "Also rare." He sat down in his chair and looked at Perrex. "What is it, Roland?"

Perrex sat up, took a deep breath and struggled out of his coat. He spread it across the back of his chair, and said, "Once more we are unemployed."

"Are you serious?"

Perrex nodded. "*Trop serieux.* They fired you a little while ago, and now I have no job."

Webster stood up. "What happened?"

Perrex looked longingly at his empty glass. "I was immersed in a discussion with that villain Henri when Hélène interrupted to say that Frederic Kaufman was calling him." He leaned forward, and struck one fist against the other palm. "Robert, I heard it all... every word. Frederic is revenging himself against you because of his *poule* of a wife. He gave Henri no reason whatever; he simply informed him that there would be no funds for the production so long as you were to be connected with it."

Robert Webster felt his body chill with the full realization of what Hildreth had done. His stomach felt as though it were shrinking to the size of a golf ball. The cigarette tasted bitter to his lips and he threw it away. Walking to the kitchen he brought back the bottle of Scotch, poured some into Roland's glass, and two fingers for himself.

When he had drunk from his glass, he said, "I don't know why I was surprised. I told her to do it. I told her to tell her husband."

"My God, are you insane?"

"Probably," Robert Webster said. "All I had to do was lay her again. She'd have gone away then and I'd have had two days to write without her bothering me."

"But you chose not to."

He looked away. "I can't explain it, Roland. It wouldn't sound logical."

"Logic is not for practical men. Illogically I broke off my association with our producers because they would do without you." He made a face. "What swine they are, those two."

"I'm sorry," Webster said. "I know what this film would have meant to you."

"*Pouf.* No more than to you." He drank from his glass and gestured at Webster's typewriter. "Still, they cannot make a picture without a story. And the story is still yours."

Webster sat down in his chair and looked at the pages he had typed. "Why should I finish it?" he asked. "What good is it now?"

Roland sat forward quickly. "Robert, listen to me. Now there is more reason than ever to finish your work. Without it you are condemned to a life of slow starvation in this garret. I can always hire myself out as a tourist spectacle or a skeleton to haunt historic chateaux, but I prefer not to. I prefer to follow my profession, just as you must follow yours."

Webster searched for a cigarette, found one, and lighted it. He gave the pack to Roland and said, "I have a contract with them."

"It is valueless. You signed some papers that they drew up, but you are not a member of the *Syndicat,* Robert, and so the contract is, unfortunately, not binding. Because my contract was still in the hands of the *Syndicat* I was able to leave their employment without professional damage."

Webster blew smoke toward the window, and said, "Could we find another producer?"

"We must."

"In France?"

Perrex shook his head. "There is nothing here for us, my friend. Everything already has been exhausted. You will agree?"

"Yes."

"So we must go elsewhere to sell our wares."

"For instance?"

"Italy, my friend. Does not its warmth and hospitality beckon to you even now? Does not its abundance of lira, of beautiful women and capable film technicians recommend itself to you at once?"

Webster nodded, thoughtfully.

Perrex finished his drink and stood up. "Good. Now you have work to do and so do I. Tonight I will write letters to friends in Rome telling them that I have decided to direct a picture in Italy and that I am attempting to persuade my friend Robert Webster to adapt his latest screenplay to an Italian background." He smiled. "We are not badly off, my friend. Between us, we have money to live for a while very comfortably on the Via Veneto. Between us we will find someone who will finance this fine story of yours. This episode will be the making of us."

Webster said, "The way you tell it, Roland, it sounds as though it's already happened."

"One must always deal in the fait accompli. That much I learned from previous dealings with producers." His face became serious, and he said, "What Frederic Kaufman did is a miserable thing, and I will see that Suzette knows he is fully responsible for frustrating her hope of fame. He may have regained his wife, Robert, but I will make very sure that he loses his mistress." His index finger touched the side of his nose. "It is done."

Roland Perrex picked up his coat, put it on, and walked to the door. "I will not bother you, Robert. When the work is finished you will call me. Then we will decide what we must do."

Robert Webster nodded and shook hands with Perrex before he closed the door. A surge of hatred rose against Hildreth, but he forced it back and thought again of Roland's words.

Lighting a cigarette Robert Webster walked back to his typewriter and looked at the blank sheet of paper. He sat down, read the last ten pages he had written, thought for a while and then began to type. He worked for half an hour, finished a scene, and then he stood up. Tilting the Scotch bottle he poured a little into his glass and drank it. He finished his cigarette, going over in his mind the episode with Hildreth and its aftermath—the decision he had reached with Roland. It's hard to take, coming from a bitch like that, he thought, but in the end it may work out for the best. If Roland can find someone in Italy to finance us we'll make the picture our own way and to hell with Kress and Gringold; Frederic and Hildreth. Particularly Hildreth.

His fingers touched the cheek she had spat on and he felt anger and resentment smoulder again. Slowly he shook his head as though he were talking aloud. I'll have to put it out of my mind, he thought. I can't keep remembering that or what happened on the beach or any of the rest of it. All of it will have to die so that I can think of other things—so the past won't weigh me down.

He thought again of Lydia's message and as he stubbed out his cigarette, he said, half-aloud, it wouldn't hurt me to see Lydia again. Now that I'm leaving Paris there's nothing I can lose by going and finding out what's on her mind. It would be a change of scene, at least, and talking with her would take my mind off things I still can't forget.

He turned out the light over his typewriter, put on his coat and locked the door behind him. A taxi drove him up the Butte of Montmartre to the Place du Tertre and when he had paid the fare he walked up the drafty staircase to Lydia's atelier.

12.

THE COOK OPENED THE DOOR, and when he went inside he saw that a fire was burning in the hearth. The big studio was warm. He took off his topcoat and laid it down on a chair, and as he walked around an easel he saw Lydia sitting in an armchair beside the fire. Her eyes looked as though she had been crying.

She turned so that she could watch him, and then she said, "I began to wonder if you were back from the Côte."

"I've been back a while." He took out a cigarette and tapped it against his thumbnail.

"Do you want a drink?"

"No, thanks." He lighted the cigarette.

"It took you a long time to decide to come here, didn't it?"

"All day."

"Are you still bitter?"

"I suppose so."

"Then why did you come at all?"

He walked toward her and sat in a chair near the fireplace. He said, "I thought Tay might be in trouble. I thought she might need help."

Lydia folded her hands in her lap, and said, "I suppose you might think that. Apparently your opinion of the Crandalls hasn't improved."

He said, "Let's not go into that. What about Tay?"

She shook her head. "No, Robert. It's about Lee." She began to dab at her eyes with a handkerchief. "Lee's left Washington with her baby. She's flying to Leopoldville to join her husband."

"Africa?" Webster asked, startled.

She nodded. "The Belgian Congo. He's to be a Civil Administrator there or something dreadful like that."

"How long have you known?"

"Only since this morning when her letter came. By now she's probably in Brussels, between planes."

"He works for his government; he goes where they send him."

"Yes. I know. But none of us thought of that when he married Lee. He seemed perfectly civilized, Robert, and we had every reason to suppose he'd be happy to stay in the United States. His father-in-law could have found a very nice position for him if he'd wanted to stay."

Webster said, "How long will they be in the Congo?"

"Five years," Lydia said. "A lifetime." She stared into the fire. "I'll never see her again, nor my great-grandchild."

Webster got up and walked to the window and looked out toward the darkening city. Near the window was a partly-finished painting of Sacré-Coeur. He said, "Lee's a grown woman. She knows what she's doing. She needed a kind of love I could never give her. If her husband could, she'd go anywhere for him."

Lydia began to cry. When the sobs stopped she dried her eyes, and said, "She was my first grandchild and I loved her very much. I still love her, though I don't suppose she means much to you by now."

He shook his head. "Not after so long," he said. "It's almost as though we were talking of someone I never knew."

"Oh, if only I could talk to her—explain in some way that would make her see how wrong it is."

"Perhaps she doesn't want to go to the Belgian Congo any more than you want her to—but she's going out of a sense of obligation to her husband, because when she married him she promised to go wherever he did. Would your talking against it help anything at all? Wouldn't it just make things harder for Lee? Wouldn't it be an injustice to her husband?"

The older woman looked at him steadily for a while, and then she said, "I'm afraid you're right, Robert. I have no business trying to run her life. It's only selfishness that makes me want to do it. Selfishness and love."

He said, "I'm sorry you didn't love Tay as much. You could have helped her by trying to guide her life."

As though she did not hear him, she said, "Please pour me a drink. I'm afraid I need one badly."

Webster went to the kitchen, made two highballs and brought them back. He gave one to Lydia.

She sipped from her glass, then looked up at him. "You want to talk about Tay, do you? All right. You were cruel to her, Robert. Yours was vicious, small-boy cruelty I didn't expect of you."

He said, "You're out of your mind."

"Am I? You hurt her and humiliated her to the extent that she's leaving France."

"Where's she going?"

"Pasadena. Where do Crandalls go when they've failed badly at something? That's where Lee went after your divorce; that's where Tay's going now."

He said, "You can't blame me for that. Not after her month on the Riviera with the wop."

Lydia shook her head. "She never went away with Rino. In fact, after meeting you, she hardly saw him again."

"I don't believe she'd leave Europe because of me."

Lydia shrugged. "You underestimate yourself. Didn't you get her letter?"

"Yes."

"But you didn't trouble to answer it. You've never even tried to see her since. That hurt her—that and the story she heard about that Kaufman woman and you."

He felt himself turn a little cold. "What story was that?"

"Oh, how the two of you were playing house; that you were even going to marry her."

Webster tilted his glass to finish his drink. "I'm not marrying Hildreth Kaufman," he said.

"I didn't suppose you would be. I thought you cared about Tay. But anyway, that's the story that got around."

"I cared for Tay more than anyone since Lee."

"But still you went away with Hildreth Kaufman." She grimaced. "You're really far more progressive than any of us, Robert, if that's how you show affection for another woman." She put down her glass and looked up at Webster. "You might just as well have whipped Tay."

He said, "That wasn't the intention. What I did shouldn't have hurt anyone at all."

Lydia snorted. "How did her husband like it?"

"He didn't."

"I thought not. You see, one never knows how something like that will turn out. The unintentional cruelties of life are sometimes the worst of all."

He said, "I'll never see Hildreth Kaufman again."

Lydia exhaled and said, "Well, I'm glad it's over. She's notorious even here in Montmartre. They warn young men against her."

"With reason," he said. "Well, I'm leaving Paris, too."

She looked up at him quickly. "Why?"

"I have to. I lost my job. I'm going to Rome to try to make a picture."

"I'm sorry, Robert. Really sorry."

"Don't be. It just happened a little while ago and I haven't made all my plans yet, but I'll be all right."

"I hope you will."

He looked at the low flames in the grate and put another piece of wood on the fire.

"Thank you, Robert. You're very thoughtful."

He brushed off his hands and began walking toward the chair where he had left his coat. "When is Tay leaving?"

"Next week. Will you see her before she goes?"

"Yes." He put on his coat.

"I'm glad of that. And I'm grateful you were able to show me I was wrong about Lee."

"I hope she'll be happy," he said. "At least give her a chance to be."

"Goodbye, Robert."

He opened the door and walked down the dark stairs to the Place du Tertre.

The wind blew raggedly across the high Butte and the park benches were empty. The trees had been stripped off most of their leaves. He looked up at the sky and saw dark clouds hanging low over the city. It felt like a snow wind.

At the Place des Saussaies he paid the taxi driver and stood for a while looking up at Tay's lighted window. Then he went into the building and walked up to her apartment.

He knocked at the door and waited until it was opened. Tay stood there, surprise on her face, and then she said, "Hello, Web."

"I just heard about Lee."

"Oh." Her voice was bitter. "You came to tell me that?"

"No." He walked through the door and into her living room.

"Why, then? Hasn't everything else already been said?"

"Not yet."

She closed the door and walked toward the piano. She said, "I'm sorry Lydia saw fit to involve you in Crandall affairs again."

"She's too old to change her habits."

"Perhaps so. And you're too damned hard even to care, aren't you?" Her voice rose a little.

"What gave you that idea?"

"The way you treated me."

"I think that's a two-way street. Lydia didn't really need me to console her over Lee's departure for the Congo. She was just making sure I knew you were leaving Paris."

She looked away from him. "I'd rather not discuss it. Why did you come here again? It wasn't to commiserate over Lee, I'm sure. She can't mean anything to you any more."

"It's time you realized that, Tay. She's your sister—but that's all she is to me. That's all she's been for a long, long time. Both of us have been shadow-boxing. Let's stop it and go somewhere for a drink and a little sensible talk."

"I've had a drink," she said, hostilely.

"Then have another. I've just had one with your grandmother, but it won't be the same as having one with you."

"No charity, Web. You know I'm leaving Paris."

He picked up her coat from a chair and brought it to her. "I'm leaving Paris, too." he said. "We'd better talk about it."

Her eyes filled with sudden tears and as he looked at her he thought that she had never been so lovely before. A lump formed in his throat as he helped her into her coat. Opening the door for her, he said, "You'll find that life can go on without Lee."

He followed her down the stairway and out to the darkness of the Place des Saussaies, and while they stood waiting for a taxi he put his arm around her to shield her from the wind.

In the taxi, she turned to him, and said, "You were on the Riviera, weren't you, Web?"

"You know I was."

"Why did you come back to Paris?"

"To finish a screenplay," he said. "Only now I'm not working for Kress and Gringold. In fact, I'm unemployed."

"Oh, Web."

"Funny how things work out," he said. "You're leaving Paris and so am I. Except for you I'm glad to be leaving. Glad to be able to stop breathing the same air as Kress and Gringold."

"You hate them, don't you?"

"I always have. I hate their smooth voices, their fake smiles, their sleek faces. I hate their lies and their exaggerations and their self-promotions. I hate people like them having anything to do with an art that's been my life."

As the taxi crossed the Pont de la Concorde, she looked out of the window and said, "I'm sorry it's been like that."

"It's my own fault," he said. "When I was in Hollywood I wrote things I should have tossed into the wastebasket. So, finally I had to work for Kress and Gringold."

"Was it because of Lee?" she asked, softly. "Was she to blame?"

"No," he said. "Not really. I let myself believe it was, but she was never to blame. Tay, she had no more maturity than a child; she had no influence on my life; on the way we lived."

"Then what was it, Web. What happened to you?"

He spread his hands and looked at them. "It was having so much money," he said, and realized that he had never admitted it to himself before. "It was making money so easily, when I'd never had money, and having someone as beautiful as Lee to spend it on. But I spent more than I made and when I was desperate I wrote badly and each time afterward what I wrote was worse." He looked at her through the cab's darkness. "That's what happened."

"I'm glad you told me," she said, quietly. "I never knew. I always thought you blamed Lee, Web. People never really know, do they?"

"No."

"I'm sorry. It can't have been pleasant for you."

"It wasn't. Small-town boy makes good. Gets the big head. Goes to hell. Cut. Print. Screen." He laughed shortly. "It's so trite I could write the story even if I hadn't lived it. You'd think I'd have realized what was happening."

"You were so very successful, Web. You would have had no reason to think it wouldn't keep on the same way."

"Thanks," he said. "Anyway, it didn't."

The taxi stopped at the entrance of the *caveau* where they had gone before, and when Webster knocked at the door she said, "It's early for this place, isn't it?"

"Yes. But they'll serve drinks."

Webster gave the doorman two hundred francs and followed Tay down the stairway into the cellar. The Negro musicians were smoking on the bandstand and talking among themselves. Only a few tables were occupied. When they were seated Tay said, "We didn't really have to come here; there were enough drinks at my apartment."

"You didn't mention it."

"Did we have to go halfway across Paris?"

"We came here the last time we were together. I thought it might be a good place to begin again." He offered her a cigarette, lighted it, and took one for himself.

Tay said, "Once I would have been interested, but no longer, Web."

"Because I didn't go to your party or answer your letter?"

"That was only a little part of it. I know you didn't because of what Lydia told you. The big thing was you going off with Hildreth Kaufman."

He said, "I'd planned that before I ever met you."

"But you could have called it off, couldn't you? Or did you run off with her to nurse your hurt feelings over me?"

"At the time it seemed the thing to do."

A waiter came and said, "Yes, sir?"

"Champagne," Webster said. "Something drinkable. We're not tourists."

"Very well, sir."

Tay said, "Now that we're on it, how *was* life on the Riviera? What was it like down there with her?"

"It was the usual," he said. "Does that satisfy you?"

"Were you going to marry her?"

He said, "I gave it some thought."

"Why?"

"She was anxious to make herself available, and she wasn't sleeping with anyone else."

"Is that your only criterion?"

"It's one of them. Not the only one."

She looked at him for a long time, and then she said, "You hypocrite. Who were you to ever question my conduct or my morals? You had no right to pass judgment on me. Your life's been no monument of purity."

"All right," he said. "Forget that part of it."

"No. I won't forget any part of it at all. You and your male ego and your damned hurt pride. Do you think you can do what you did and then just wipe the slate clean?"

"I'd like to."

She began to speak but the waiter came, opened the champagne, and poured a glass for himself. He sipped it and said to Webster, "It is an excellent *cuvée, m'sieu,* and not at all what you feared it might be." He finished the glass, then filled Tay's and Webster's. The band at the end of the cellar began to play; unobtrusively, as though it were the end of the night instead of only the beginning.

Webster said, "You shouldn't give up your job, Tay. There's no reason for you to leave Paris. You were happy here before you met me."

"I was, wasn't I? But you changed Paris for me. At first Paris was wonderful and exciting but you made it seem shabby and sensual and you shamed me. Thanks a lot, Web; you did that much for me."

He said, "I had no right to."

"Did you think having been married to Lee gave you the right? Well, maybe I did, too. I worried a lot about what you'd been to Lee when I first met you." She laughed abruptly. "I was measuring myself for a large-size guilt complex." She drank from her glass and watched two couples beginning to dance. Then she said, "You expected a lot of me, Web. Too much. Too damn much for anyone. You thought I should be just the same as I was when I was a girl in Pasadena. You thought I was obligated to stay always as I was when I was young."

"I knew a lot of girls when they were young; but now youth turns out to be only a temporary condition. I've learned that when girls grow older they stop being virgins."

She said, slowly, "I did you no wrong."

"You killed some of my illusions, and at my age they die hard."

She said, quietly, "I had some illusions about you, too. And you managed to kill them."

"We suffered the disadvantage of having known each other once before."

She tilted the glass toward her lips, drank, and said, "You've had the emotional education of two Crandall sisters, Web. That's quite an accomplishment, isn't it?"

"Depends on how you look at it."

"Yes, I suppose it does. Well, that's how I look at it." She finished her glass and revolved it between her fingers. "It was lousy luck meeting you again. I was reasonably happy in my own way. Why did it have to be changed by you?"

He said, "Have you lost so much?"

She looked toward the dance floor, and said, "Dance with me before I cry."

"All right." He stood up and held back her chair. Then he followed her to the dance floor, and when she stopped and turned to face him her lips brushed his cheek unintentionally. He took her in his arms, and they began to dance slowly, in rhythm with the music. At first her body was stiff and awkwardly responding, but in a little while he could feel its suppleness return, and he said, "Feeling better now?"

"Yes."

"Want to stay here?"

He felt her shake her head. When the music ended, they went back to the table and the waiter filled their glasses again. Tay drank, put down her glass, and said, "This doesn't solve anything at all."

"No."

"Not even if we were drunk."

"Not even if we drank all night."

She looked at him, and said, "Oh, Web, I feel like absolute hell."

"So do I."

"I didn't ask to be born Lee's sister."

"It's time you forgot it." He called the waiter and paid for the champagne. The waiter filled their glasses again and Webster said, "Our first trouble was thinking we knew each other better than we really did."

"Yes."

"But we didn't know each other at all."

"I kept on thinking of you the way I always had—until I heard about you and Hildreth Kaufman." She drank from her glass, and said, "What happened to that?"

"It makes a long story. Not a pretty one."

She looked at him, and said, "She's beautiful, isn't she, Web? And very rich and experienced."

"I don't want to talk about her."

"When did you see her last?" she persisted.

He took a deep breath. "Today," he said. "About four hours ago."

"You bastard!" She started to get up from the table but his hand held her wrist and he said, "I sent her away. I didn't want her."

She turned to face him and her mouth was bitter. "Once you did."

"Yes," he said. "For a while." He got up from the table and pulled back her chair. He helped her into her coat and then they walked up the stairway and out of the big iron-shod door onto the Rue St. Benoît. He opened the door of a waiting taxi and they got inside.

In Tay's apartment Webster sat at the piano bench and watched her carry Scotch and ice and Vittel to the table. She said,

"I suppose Scotch is all right after champagne." She made two highballs carefully and brought one to him. He took it from her, and said, "I don't want you to leave Europe, Tay."

"Well, she said, "I'm going back, anyway."

"Why?"

"It's better if I do."

He shook his head. "That's no answer."

"Then play for me." She moved against the piano and leaned forward so that she could see his face. When his hands did not move, she said, "All right. There's something between us, Web, and we know it. But we can't hurry it this time. I'll go back home. If you still think there's something when your picture's finished, I'll come back to Paris."

He said, "I'm leaving Paris, too. I told you that but I didn't tell you why."

"No."

He ran one hand through his hair and looked away from her. His throat felt dry even after the drinks, and he began to talk slowly at first; until he was sure of himself. Then he turned to watch her face while he told her what had happened during the afternoon.

When he had finished she stood up, walked to the table, and made another drink for herself. She said, "Do you think Roland Perrex can find money for the picture?"

"He says he can."

"What if he can't, Web? I couldn't stand you not having it work out."

He shrugged. "I have to take the chance."

She came toward him and he felt her hands touch the sides of his face. "Yes," she said, softly. "It's what you have to do."

When he looked up he saw that her lips were very close to his. He took her hands and drew her down beside him. He kissed her lips and they were full and open, and when she drew away, she said, "Oh, Web, why didn't you ask me to go away with you?"

"There wasn't time."

"Do you think I'd have gone with you?"

He smiled and kissed her lips again. "I think so."

"Why? I didn't go with Rino."

"That was different."

"Don't be so sure," she said, and let herself be kissed again.

He breathed deeply, and said, "The difference is that I love you." He drew her body against his, and said, "I think you love me."

When she answered he could feel tears on her cheeks and her voice sounded like a little girl's. "I do, darling. Oh, Web, I've loved you for a long time. Incestuously at first, I guess, but now I don't even care. You're the only one I could ever love. I couldn't bear it if you left me."

"I won't."

Without realizing it, he was standing up, taking her hand and drawing her toward the hallway that opened into her darkened bedroom. He sat down on the bed and his hands brought her to him, and their lips met. Then it was as though he were being drawn into a pool of liquid fire until he was utterly immersed in its heat.

Later, Tay said, "Ah, Web, you make me so grateful. So wonderfully grateful."

"Don't talk now."

"No."

He felt drowsy. Beside him her body was a dying flame.

She said, "Wherever you go I'll go with you."

"Yes."

"All my life I've loved you and wanted you. Always. Did you know?"

His eyes felt tired and his body was completely relaxed.

"You didn't ever love Hildreth Kaufman, did you?" she asked.

"No."

He fell asleep then and when he opened his eyes he saw the shadow of her body sitting beside him. He reached out to touch her, to convince himself of her reality, and she said, “Don’t wake, darling. I was only watching you.”

“What were you thinking.”

She stroked his forehead, and said, “Web, you’ll take me to places where you’ve never been with anyone.”

“Yes; we’ll go to Venice and have good times on the Lido.”

“Or Portofino—I’ve never been there. But later, in the summer.”

He nodded and looked up at her profile. “You’re very beautiful, my love.”

“I want to be; so you’ll never want to make love with anyone else.” She leaned over to kiss him, and her breasts swung downward to brush lightly against his chest. “I’ll sleep wonderfully tonight. You’ve done that for me. Ah, darling, to think I never knew how making love with you would be.”

“I’ll sleep well, too.”

“Do you want a drink or a cigarette or anything?”

“Only if you do.”

She got up from the bed and he saw the small-girl waist and the beautifully rounded back and the fineness of her flanks. She took a dressing gown from the closet and put it on. As she fluffed back her hair, she said, “Tomorrow we won’t go anywhere, will we?”

“No. We’ll stay here all day.”

“That’s what I want to do. And in the morning I’ll wake beside you for the first time.”

She leaned over to kiss him again, before she went out of the room.

When she had gone he lay quietly, his mind beyond thought or motion, listening to the sound of the wind in the trees outside; watching the shadow patterns of moving branches against the walls of the room.

He closed his eyes, feeling secure, finally, because he was in her room, insulated from the world outside, and when she came back he was asleep. While she lay beside him finishing a cigarette, she watched the first few flakes of snow glance off the window pane. A flurry whirled against the window, making the night opaque with whiteness. Outside in the Place des Saussaies the level of the fallen snow began to rise until the frozen ground was covered and drifts formed along the curb and in the corners of the doorways.

For Paris it was an early snow. It was the earliest fall of snow since the war, and long before dawn the streets of the quiet city were covered with white.

THE END

www.ingramcontent.com/pod-product-compliance
Lightning Source LLC
Chambersburg PA
CBHW022159240626
47153CB00007B/2731
9781952138638